I0670864

Humorous Fiction
in the grand tradition.

Me and Aunt Izzy

What the reviewers say:

- "Kansas readers already know that Max Yoho
  is a literary treasure, and he has the awards to
  prove it. Now it's time for the rest of the world to
  discover this masterful story teller. His characters
  are delightfully quirky and lovable, storylines
  one-of-a-kind, and writing style generously laced
  with joyful humor. **Me and Aunt Izzy** is delightful,
  humorous, joyful, and highly recommended."

  — **Laurel Johnson,** *Midwest Book Review*

- "Given the names, Queen Isabella of Spain, and
  her nephew, Jefferson Davis Johnson, you would
  expect a prim and proper look at life in southeast Kansas, but life is full of surprises in this
  delightful book, set in Jesse James' old stomping
  grounds."

  — **Jeff Imparato**, Public Services Librarian

- "Yoho delivers yet another bildungsroman filled
  with farcical characters and zany antics. Sure to
  induce spit takes if you are foolhardy enough to
  eat and drink while reading this book."

  — **Carol Ann Robb**, Book Wrangler,
  Pittsburg ("Armageddon") Public Library

Also by Max Yoho:

The Revival
Tales from Comanche County
Felicia, These Fish Are Delicious
The Moon Butter Route
With the Wisdom of Owls

Me
and
Aunt Izzy

*Doing Time at the Jesse James
Hideout and Coal Mining Company*

Me
and
Aunt Izzy

*Doing Time at the Jesse James
Hideout and Coal Mining Company*

Max Yoho

Dancing Goat Press
Topeka, Kansas

Me and Aunt Izzy

Copyright © 2011 by Max Yoho

Reproduction in any manner, in whole or in part,
in English or in other languages, or otherwise
without written permission of the publisher is prohibited.

This is a work of fiction.
All characters and events portrayed in this book are fictional,
and any resemblance to real people or incidents is purely coincidental.

For Information address: Dancing Goat Press
3013 SW Quail Creek Dr., Topeka, Kansas 66614

www.dancinggoatpress.com

ISBN: 0970816065
EAN 13: 978-0970816061

PRINTED IN THE UNITED STATES OF AMERICA

For Carol
and my sons, Alex, Stuart and Nick.

With special thanks to
my editor, Morgan Chilson.

And thanks also to
Queen Elizabeth, Pope John Paul II,
J.K. Rawlings and Lady Gaga
for staying out of my way.

1

Great Aunt Queen Isabella of Spain Johnson waited inside the screen door, her nose pressed against the little rusty squares. At her age, she should have known better.

We'd just arrived in our 1938 Hudson Terraplane, and I likely set a new world record for a boy opening a car door slowly. As far as I was concerned, I would wait for a new ice age before I actually got out. I stalled. "Do they really handle snakes at her church?" I asked my dad.

"That's what I've heard," he told me with a revengeful grin. "But don't worry, you'll be in Sunday School with the other kids, and they'll likely just start you practicing with fishing worms."

If that was supposed to cheer me up, it was terrible inadequate.

I had promised to be on my best behavior during my stay here, but if anyone believed Jefferson Davis Johnson would kneel at an altar while a rattlesnake licked his chops for a tasty butt-bite, they were flat mistaken.

A tumbling-down sign in the front yard declared this to be "The Jesse James Hideout and Coal Mining Co." That, at least, promised a little excitement. Maybe my visit wouldn't be all torture and slavery.

It wasn't that Great Aunt Queen Isabella of Spain actually ran a home for boys who had accidentally burned down their parents' privies; it was more like...well, my mom said it this way, "Maybe we all needed a vacation." That's fine and dandy, but I noticed no one's suitcase got packed but mine!

Maybe, just maybe, spending a week or two at Great Aunt Queen Isabella of Spain's place was better than reform school. Likely better than being sent to Leavenworth prison. Still and all, it wasn't how I'd planned to spend my summer vacation.

My complete failure to master the art of multiplication hadn't exactly endeared me to my family either, but I was somewhat rescued from that fiasco by my enthusiasm to learn a new word every day. For instance, take the word "fiasco": a fiasco is when you plan something and it goes so wrong you just want to go off and molder in your grave for a while. The opposite of the word "fiasco" is "antonym," which means that you finally got something right.

I choose my Daily Word by opening my dictionary and, with my eyes closed, I point to a word. This is called "random." A random can be a dangerous way to do business because once I pointed at "rattlesnake."

Now see, I want you to understand this whole dang mess with the privy was not my fault. If anybody ought to get the blame for burning down the privy, it's the dumb school! If anyone ever asks me, "Which is more important for a boy to learn: How to spell the word 'Constantinople'?—or—Should a fellow ever try to roll a cigar out of toilet paper and dried dock weed leaves?" I just guess you know what I'll tell them! And I'll show them my burnt off eyebrows and the ashes of the privy to prove it.

Anyway, has anyone ever really been requested to spell "Constantinople"? "Requested" just means "asked" to, and is used to show people that you know two different ways to say the same thing.

My dad grabbed my brown, cardboard suitcase and nudged me toward the front porch. He reminded me, one more time, that if I broke my glasses it would be for the third time, and by state law I would have to go to reform school.

Great Aunt Queen Isabella of Spain stepped out the door and, just like I figured would happen, she had little rusty squares of screen door printed on the end of her nose. She stood straight and tall, and looked to be all business—the kind of person who subscribes to the *Kansas City Star*, and not just the Sunday paper, either.

My dad maintains that Great Aunt Queen Isabella of Spain is the most dignified of all the Johnson women. He says she is wise and calls her the family "Matriarch."

He said I could learn a lot from her—and I did. The sight of her was a lesson to me. If I grow up to be a Matriarch I will darn sure wipe my nose off before I step out a screen door.

Great Aunt Queen Isabella of Spain lived at the south edge of Armageddon, just a few miles from our little town of Epic, in Southeast Kansas. Our whole area is called the "Little Balkans" because that's what Governor Walter Stubbs named it. My dad says Walt was a good, sound Republican. He says a damn Democrat would have never had the wit to think of such a name.

Anyway, when she stepped out from behind that

screen door she looked meaner than I remembered. I knew my dad had called her "dignified" because he was too polite to say "ugly." He was right about one thing though, she fair bristled with Matriarch. She was as ugly as Abraham Lincoln and nearly as tall, but there was no trace of kindness in her black little eyes, and I knew she wouldn't free the slaves in a million years.

I know about Abraham Lincoln and George Washington because their pictures hang on two sides of my schoolroom, and if you try to cheat on your multiplications they make you feel as uncomfortable as a Bad Example.

Aunt Queen Isabella of Spain's hair was pulled tight into a ball at the back, top-part of her head, about the size of a little hedge ball except that it wasn't green. It made her eyes sort of squint like that Chinaman on our checkerboard. Her dress was long, and as gray as a reform school wall.

"So, Little Willard," she hollered at my dad, "is this the bad boy who burned down your crapper?" I felt my face go red all over at the thought that this old lady, who fair wafted of the aroma of Matriarch, would use such an ungainly word.

"Little Willard" is what most of the family call my dad, so as to tell him from his uncle who was Great Aunt Queen Isabella of Spain's brother. It never made much sense to me, because the old Willard was dead and it shouldn't be too hard to guess which Willard was asking, "Please pass the Grape Nuts."

Great Uncle dead Willard had made a fortune right there at home from the Jesse James Hideout and Coal Mining Company, so three of his nephews, right off, got named Willard.

Welcome to the Johnson family.

"This is the one," my dad told her, "and he has

caused great embarrassment to Ida, who has to go over to the DeCastro's to 'visit Mrs. Jones.'"

Now, see, "Ida" is my mom's name, although I don't know why, and "visiting Mrs. Jones" just means she has to pee, although she'd rather die than say so because she's a woman. Anyway, you can't blame her for not wanting to go to an Italian's house to pee.

"Well, we'll take care of that little problem," Great Aunt Queen Isabella of Spain promised. She didn't mean the problem of having to pee in an Italian's house; she meant the problem of me burning down privies.

I guarantee that word "we" sent a wooly worm crawling up my back! My teacher says only a king or the Pope can call himself "we." I tried to look behind her to see if there was a king or the Pope hiding there, but there was just a cat. The only other thing I could figure was that the poor old Pope was tied up in the dungeon waiting to be punished for burning down the Papal Privy.

"Well, come on in out of the sun and have some lemonade," she commanded. So we did: my dad, me, and more cats than I have ever seen in one place and at one time.

"Do all these cats have names?" I requested.

"Of course they do. They are all named Rudolph. This one is 'Rudolph Valentino.' This one is 'Rudy Vallee.' This little rascal is 'Prince Rudolph the 2nd of Heidelberg.' This one is 'Willamina Rudolph, the Lost Dauphin of Herzegovina,'"—and on and on she Rudolphed—until she had a whole plethora of Rudolphs. A "plethora" is what happens when you get so much of a thing that it will probably go bad before you can possibly use it all up.

My dad had warned me about Great Aunt Queen Isabella of Spain's lemonade. He said she had used the same lemon for at least forty years. He said a lemon would last a long time if you just tied a string around it and dragged it through a pitcher of ice water. I believe he was right.

Anyway, Great Aunt Queen Isabella of Spain led us all through a beaded curtain and into the parlor where we settled in. I took a good look at the furniture because my dad had ranted about it all the way down here. It was one of his favorite rants, and he was good at it. "...and then when Uncle Willard died she just threw all that fine old furniture away. Most likely she burned it. She hired some jake-leg carpenter to nail a bunch of oak boards together and called it 'Mission style.' Ugliest stuff I've ever seen. Not a graceful carved scroll or acanthus leaf on any of it."

Dad chose a wicker armchair which, I guess he figured, wouldn't be an insult to his butt. I sat myself in an oak rocker. There was an Atwater Kent radio and a Victrola and a lamp with a nice dangle of beads as a fringe on the shade. A Chickering player piano with a butt-worn bench almost begged me to give it a try, but I didn't dare.

Great Aunt Queen Isabella of Spain gave us each a glass of lemonade and passed around a plate of cucumber sandwiches, all cut up into little triangles. "Oh gracious," my dad said. He picked one up with his fat, stubby fingers. "You always remember how I love these." With his pinky finger pointing out, he admired that stupid sandwich like it was the Hopeful diamond. Great Aunt Queen Isabella of Spain smiled a tight-mouthed smile and sat herself primly on the edge of a straight-backed oak chair. "Primly" is how you sit if you want to make everyone else uncomfortable and feel as if they have a boogers hanging out of their noses.

"Well, Ida wrote me that you have a new minister there in Epic. How do you like him?"

"I'm not sure yet," my dad told her. "On his first Sunday, attendance was up four percent just because everybody wanted to see what he was like. The collection came in at $17.38, which equals .96555 per worshiper, plus my two dollars, which brought the total to $19.38. That's roughly parallel to the attendance, as it should be. All in all, I was pleased. I don't know how much the Methodists and the Baptists brought in because they haven't made their deposits yet, but I'll find out. I don't have any idea how much the Catholics make on a Sunday. They do their banking here in Armageddon, but I expect it's quite a lot. I suppose it costs a lot to keep all those statues painted up." He chuckled—alone. "Well, I guess it takes all kinds, and they do pay their taxes.

"But this new preacher preached against usury, which makes me think he doesn't understand much about the banking business. Anyway, who does he think puts two dollars in the collection plate every Sunday of the year, come rain or come shine? Some people don't seem to realize that without banks this old world would just grind to a halt."

Great Aunt Queen Isabella of Spain said, "You are a good man, Little Willard. I'm sure your heavenly reward will be great. Maybe ten percent on your earthly investment."

My dad tried to look humble, but I don't believe he gets enough practice to really carry it off.

"Well, that's nice, I declare. Would you care for more lemonade, Little Willard?"

He told her he'd had about enough and said he really needed to get back to the bank. "Ada and I really appreciate you taking on this little problem of ours though. We're sure your good influence will be a lasting...ah...influence on our progen, as he...ah... embraces toward manhood."

"On your *what?*" Aunt Izzy asked.

"Our progen," Dad explained. "You know, two or more kids are progeny. We only got one, our 'progen.'"

My dad had gone to Business College, and it was mighty hard to get ahead of him.

2

As we walked my dad to the car, he gave Great Aunt Queen Isabella of Spain one last warning: "Give that boy a handful of sand, and he'll find a way to break it!"

When he'd pulled his shiny new Hudson Terraplane out of the driveway and back onto the gravel road we headed back indoors. There Great Aunt Queen Isabella of Spain whirled around, untied her sensible shoes, and kicked them across the room. "Twenty-three Skidoo! You old fuddy-duddy," she cried. "I'm sorry, Jeffie, but your old man is an old fuddy-duddy. He was a fuddy-duddy as a chrysalis and he has been a fuddy-duddy from babyhood to manhood. Did you see his face when I handed him that glass of lemonade? He hates my lemonade!

"You know how I make it? Just for him? I tie a string around a lemon and drag it through a pitcher of ice water. Lord, he hates my lemonade! And those little triangle cucumber sandwiches? He hates them more than he hates my lemonade! You could almost see his butt clinch up when he took one."

She opened a drawer and took out a pack of cigarettes, slipped one into a long, ivory holder, and lit it with a shiny gold lighter. The smoke rolled out her nose.

Was I in a time warp? Another galaxy? Even Buck Rogers had never come up against anything like this!

Then, with the cigarette holder still between her lips and her eyes all asquint to keep the smoke out, she reached up and started removing the pins from her hair. Now here's a funny thing: with her shoes off and her hair down, Great Aunt Queen Isabella of Spain had lost most of her ugly; and she didn't look mean. I'm not going to claim she was about to be crowned "Miss Armageddon of 1938." Still and all, I knew I had been a little wrong. I had judged her to be about one hundred and twelve years old, but with her hair all down around her shoulders, I swear, she could pass for seventy-five!

I guess I was still standing there with my mouth open, caused by her previous outrageous extravaganza. She grinned and said, "Come on, Jeffie, close your mouth; the flies will get in. I'll get you some real lemonade."

I followed her into the kitchen—along with the plethora of cats—and watched while she squeezed a few lemons and made a pitcher of the real thing. The ice pick lay handy, right atop the big chunk of ice in the top of the icebox. Aunt Izzy hacked and slivered ice into the pitcher.

I guess my Christian upbringing was not completely shattered until she pulled a bottle from the cupboard and poured a good amount into her glass. "I like a little giggle juice in mine," she admitted. "I guess I'd better not offer you any, you might get all snockered up and go out and burn my shithouse down."

Well, I know I turned red all over, and felt about as small as an amoeba. An "amoeba" is sort of a little bug that's so tiny you can't see it, so you just have to have faith in the veracity of your dictionary. "Veracity" means truth, so if your dictionary doesn't have veracity, then I guess you are just out one amoeba. Anyway, amoebas don't have mothers or fathers like most people, they divide themselves—if you can believe that.

"Oh, Jeffie," she said, "don't look so embarrassed, I'm joshing you. Hell, maybe I'll be the one who gets snockered and burn my own shithouse down!"

I was completely nonplused. "Nonplused" means that maybe somebody knew what was going on, but it sure as heck wasn't me. I wanted to change the subject.

"Great Aunt Queen Isabella of Spain, ma'am, I..."

"For crying out loud, Jeffie, cut out that 'Queen la de da crap.' Just call me Izzy! Now what were you going to say?"

"Well, Ma'am—er—Izzy, I guess I've always wondered how you came to be named that... name."

"I'm not surprised, kiddo. Everyone asks about that. I guess it's a funny story—kinda. Actually, your old fuddy-duddy-daddy is the only one who ever calls me that. But here's the way it happened: on the day I was born, my daddy came home ab-so-lute-ly snockered. Wait a minute! You like to learn new words don't you? Let's do it this way. First we'll start a sentence:

My daddy came home (choose one):
- snockered
- ossified

- splifficated
- bombed
- plastered

Do you like those words, Jeffie? I got a million of 'em."

"Does that mean he was drunk?"

"Yes, sir, he was so drunk he didn't have a clue."

"Might we say he was—nonplused?"

"Kiddo, that big Palooka was nonplused to the gills! So anyway, the doctor says to him, 'What shall I write down as this girl child's name?' And my daddy says, 'Hell, I don't care.' And just off the top of his head, he says 'How about Queen Isabella of Spain?' And so that's what the doctor wrote down, and that's what my daddy wrote in the family Bible."

"Holy cow! Was that name okay with your mom?"

Aunt Izzy splashed herself a little more giggle juice, and considered.

"Not exactly," she finally answered. "She fired three shots at daddy from his own gat, but she was still a little weakened from childbirth, so she missed him every shot."

"Gat?" I interrogated.

"Sure, you know, 'gat,' 'heater,' 'iron,' 'chopper,' 'rod.' Boy, for a kid who plans to learn a new word every day...it's a good thing you've got a lot of days ahead of you.

"Look here. Let me use it in a sentence: 'The grand piano bimbo raised his gat and blasted that grifter into next Thursday.'"

"Wow!" I exalted to her. "Let me write all this down." Aunt Izzy brought me a pencil and paper.

"Now...talk some more. Please."

"Well then, you might say, 'Then he put him in a concrete kimono and tossed him into the deep briny.'

"Anyway, Jeffie, this morning I chopped the head off an old sunrise squawker, and I'd better get started frying him up. So why don't you just go outside and look around while I get dinner? *Capish-avous?*"

Now, I'll tell you for sure, my old head was starting to get dizzy from too much nonplusity. The only understandable thing I garnered from that last bit was the sound of the question mark. So I just took a shot in the dark, and said, "No, Ma'am. I went before we started down here."

Aunt Izzy gave me the kind of look I had sort of gotten used to since I burned down the privy, but then she grinned big at me and said, "Jefferson, you are just a regular lollapalooza."

So, like she told me, I went out the back door to have a look around. I was accompanied by twelve hundred Rudolphs—give or take only one or two. In case you have been thwarted from such an experience, I will tell you it's like walking through a cyclone of fur. Except I don't guess a cyclone "merowers" when you step on one.

Great Aunt Queen...I mean, Izzy, told me not to go near the old mine. Now, here's a funny thing: before she mentioned that old mine it never occurred to me. But now, it just seemed like there wasn't much reason to go on living if I didn't go there. Still and all, I'd made a vow to keep out of trouble and, if there is anything that will get a fellow in more trouble than burning down a privy, it's breaking a vow.

So I headed in the direction of the barn, parting the Rudolphs like old Moses parted the Red Sea, except my particular sea wasn't red. It was what you might call "motley."

I know the word "motley" twice as well as I know other words because I randomed it several times. My old dictionary had got wet on some of the "M" part, and some of the pages were a little warped and stuck together.. If you're not careful you could random "motley" thirteen or fourteen times in a row.

You probably won't believe me, and I don't blame you, but it's the honest veracity. I admit this is the first time I've used that word because, if anything is more motley than twelve hundred cats, I just wish someone would tell me what.

Anyway, I opened that big barn door and there sat Great Uncle dead Willard's Pierce Arrow car. It seemed as big as a locomotive, and it was a beaut! It was what they call a "thing of beauty and a joy forever." I expect old Great Uncle Willard felt pretty forlorn, having that fine car just sitting there—what with him being dead and all.

His old McClellan saddle lay, shamefully, in a heap on the floor. My dad told me about that saddle. Great Uncle Willard rode clear across France on it in the Great War. The government asked him to go over and shoot the Kaiser and, if the darned old Kaiser had held still, I expect he would have. But now it was all covered with bird poop. The saddle, not the Kaiser.

Right beside the saddle was a big trunk-like box and it was covered with bird poop too. I guess you can't expect a dumb bird to hit the saddle every time. Anyway, if I ever hoped to find a treasure trove, I knew this was it. I have never randomed the word "trove," but I'm pretty sure it would behoove me to do it pretty quick. If I get me a treasure, I'd feel pretty silly just standing there letting it splatter all over the floor because I didn't have a trove. Behoove means something you *really* should do, like taking Milk of Magnesia.

In fairness to me, I will tell you that big old trove had no lock on it or any sign saying NO TRESPASSING.

I know it's wrong to snoop into other people's things, but I consoled my conscience that it wouldn't hurt anything to take one little peek. I promised not to touch any of the gold or pearls or diamonds. Anyway, there wasn't anyone around to see me. I figured if God looked down on me and thought I was doing wrong, He could just send a bird to poop on me and I'd close the lid right back up and no harm done.

Well, sir, it plain doesn't work to open a trove just a crack. I have found that, as a general rule, troves are dark as the inside of a cow. So I opened it all the way, and then slammed it shut as fast as I could and peed myself. Just a little bit.

Even old Hopalong Cassidy would have peed himself if he'd seen those big old round skull eyes looking up at him!

Then I thought: what if I had discovered a murder? If I solved the wicked crime and brought the offensive villain to justice, I would be a hero. They would give me a medal and take my picture and put it on the front page of *The Buffalo County Trans-Weekly Disciplinarian*. To reopen the trunk was my duty, plain and simple.

"Duty" is what you do because you have to, even though you're likely to be sorry. "Behoove" can't be used as a substitute for Duty even though you know that Duty is going to be worse than poison ivy.

I took a deep breath, promised myself I would stand there like an Onward Christian Soldier, and flung the lid open.

I didn't run and I didn't scream because, woe and behold, it was a stupid old gas mask staring at me. Be that as it may, I turned those glassy eyes away. It wasn't that those eyes really spooked me, but I know it's not polite to stare and it seemed to behoove me to spare it some embarrassment if I could.

Still and all, I felt pretty good about myself. It *coulda* been a dead skull! And it was a trove full of treasure. Besides the gas mask there was a German helmet with a spike on top for butting some enemy in the belly. There was a bayonet that was a knife on one side and a jagged saw-thing on the other. It would hurt like sin if you got poked with it.

I admit I broke my promise about not touching anything, but it wasn't my fault. This wasn't your normal treasure. It wasn't just a bunch of diamonds and rubies and girl-stuff like that. It's near impossible to keep your hands off a thing that is a knife on one side and a saw on the other.

And, folded up all neatly, was Great Uncle Willard's old soldier coat. I think they are called "tunics"— probably because a long time ago a bunch of A-rabs or somebody got in a fight over a jacket and called it the Tunic Wars. And then, of course, if you remember, there was old Joseph in the Bible who had a "coat of many colors" which was, likely, a tunic. But it didn't matter because his brothers got together and threw him in the well for his trouble. The coat was probably "motley," too, but people weren't very smart in those olden days, and maybe "motley" hadn't been invented yet. I hope they were smart enough to take the coat off him before they threw him in the well.

Anyway, I kind of nuzzled the coat out of the way so as not to get throwed in a well, even though I don't have any brothers. And there, right underneath it, was another little trove. It was just a cardboard box trove, so I wasn't expecting much. But the first treasure I saw was some French "franks." "Franks" are what the French people call their money, which, I suppose, makes as much sense as calling all of your cats "Rudolph."

But under the franks I found the real treasure: a whole stack of picture postcards. And, Judas Priest, they were dynamite! Now, I knew what the war was all about—and it wasn't about some stupid coat. That doggoned Kaiser had wanted these postcards all for himself. Every one was the picture of a woman, and you wouldn't believe it—there wasn't a stitch of clothing among the whole stack. You could even see their bellybuttons!

I wiped the unaccountable steam from my glasses and then did a quick check to make sure I was alone. If I got caught looking at these pictures they would likely take away every one of my Sunday School perfect attendance medals!

Just then Aunt Izzy clanged the supper bell and I jumped a mile. It near scared me to death. As fast as I could, I put everything back like I found it and even scooped up a handful of bird poop for the top of the trove.

I ran back to the house, tripping a few times over the furry plethora, with the memory of those ladies' kind smiles clogging my brain.

3

I guess nobody in the world can fry a "sunrise squawker" as good as Aunt Izzy. My mom would have died of embarrassment at how much I ate. I believe nothing in the world gives a fellow an appetite like seeing a stack of naked French ladies. But Aunt Izzy didn't seem to mind at all how much I gobbled. She said she just loved to see a boy enjoy his food. I wanted to tell her that all she had to do was keep a few naked French ladies handy. But I didn't.

Sitting there eating with Aunt Izzy was just fine with me. She never once brought up a mention of burning outhouses or hinted that learning the multiplication tables was the next best thing to going to heaven.

With Aunt Izzy, everything was the "bee's knees," or a "lollapalooza." And if a stupid old privy happened to accidentally go up in smoke, it was "pure copacetic" with her.

I pushed the last of the peas around on my plate and sort of looked at her.

"I saw Great Uncle Willard's Pierce Arrow," I admitted.

"Oh, yeah," she smiled, "Waja think of that old hoopie?"

"It's a real 'lollypulooskie,'" I told her.

"We'll have to work a little on that word," she laughed. "That'll be your word for tomorrow. That car really is the cat's pajamas, though.

"Hey, Jeffie, butt me, if you would be so kind."

I thought of that old spiky German helmet out in the trove, but, holy cow, I wouldn't butt Aunt Izzy with that for a million dollars. I guess I must have been looking pretty dumb, because she laughed out loud again. "Right there by your elbow—you know, my ciggies. I'd get 'em myself, but my dogs are about to kill me!"

There was no doubt about it, these Armageddon people spoke a whole 'nother language than us Presbyterians.

When I finally got the "killer dogs" and the "ciggies" sorted out in my mind, I passed them to her. The ciggies. She fit one into her ivory holder and, still grinning at me, let the smoke swirl out her nose. Actually, she seemed to grin at me a lot, and shake her head in disbelief a lot too. I guess she just wasn't used to having company around.

She tapped the ash into her plate without a thought, and my mom would have died if she had seen that!

"Seems like your daddy takes his church-going pretty seriously," she said.

"Oh, he does," I told her. "We all have to go every Sunday because it's a behoove. He says a banker and his family have to set an example for the rest of the world. He says it's really important to go, now that he's church treasurer. He says anybody who doesn't believe in God...just send them to him and he'll show them the deposit slips."

Aunt Izzy ridded the table and started washing the dishes. I volunteered to dry.

"Aunt Izzy, my dad says the people in your church handle snakes. Is that true?"

"Handle snakes? Jesus Christ, Jefferson, did your dad really tell you that? I wouldn't touch a snake if my life depended on it! Your father is a plain and simple prevaricator!"

"No, ma'am," I told her. "He's a plain and simple Presbyterian. We all are. The whole family."

She reached down a glass and a half-full Mason jar of clear liquid from the kitchen cabinet. Then she poured herself about a half glass full.

"I'll need a little coffin varnish to wash *that* one down," she said.

I guess if she really had a coffin in her belly it got plenty varnished.

"Snakes? Indeed!" She sputtered a little and took another sip. When I got a whiff of that "coffin varnish," I knew Aunt Izzy wasn't going to die of snakebite. Not tonight, anyway.

She tousled my hair with her soapy hand and an errant drop tickled down behind my left ear. An "errant" is something that wanders around looking for adventure. As far as I know, there isn't much adventure hiding behind my left ear.

She wiped out the cast iron skillet and set it aside. I dried the last plate and put it in the cabinet.

"It's about time for Fibber McGee," she said. "Let's go in the other room and turn on the radio."

The old Atwater Kent whizzled and screeched but, by and by, old Harlow Wilcox, who was so fond of Johnson's Wax, declared, "Fibber McGee."

Now I guess old Fibber and Molly are about the

funniest people on earth, and we were still hooting with laughter when Harlow made his final recommendation. Aunt Izzy decided to have another "little drinky poo" to wash away the giggles. It didn't work.

It was nice to have an Aunt Izzy who giggled instead of an Aunt Izzy with rusty squares on her nose, looking like the Grim Reaper. Still, it was also a little embarrassing.

I knew it was my behoovement to get her mind off Fibber, so I said, "Aunt Izzy, tell me about the old mine." Well, sir, her old mouth snapped shut and, if there was a giggle on its way out, I just expect it got chomped in two.

She frowned and said, "Well, Jefferson, there is really nothing to tell. It's just an old hole in the ground. I believe it's time for bed."

We went upstairs and she showed me where my bedroom was. She turned back the covers, but somehow she was being too polite. There was something like ozone in the air. The dictionary claims ozone is an "allotrope," and that's what it smells like too. I haven't yet randomed "allotrope." But it sounds part alligator and part antelope, so I guess I shouldn't be surprised if it stinks.

Still and all, ozones and allotropes seem to make a fellow feel guilty as heck. Anyway, I'm not going to do any more behooves by mentioning the mine to Aunt Izzy.

My dad would have killed me if he had known, but I didn't say my prayers before I went to bed. I didn't ask any "please blesses" on anybody and, if anybody asked a "please bless Jefferson Davis Johnson" on me, I would be very much surprised.

I also did not ask God for another Great War to happen when I grow up, but I would really like to go to France.

I believe there really *are* French ladies or there wouldn't be pictures of them.

I have never seen a picture of God.

4

Aunt Izzy's place is not exactly a farm; it's more long and more skinny. A hole-in-the-ground coal mine doesn't take much room. You can see her neighbors' houses on both sides. The one on the east belongs to Mrs. Potts, who is a widow because her husband stepped in front of a train. Aunt Izzy says it was an accident, but I haven't met Mrs. Potts yet. She has two daughters (Mrs. Potts, not Aunt Izzy) named "Lucille" and "Pauline." Girls are a bane. A "bane" is about the same as a pain except you can't take an aspirin and make it go away.

Mister Eugene and Mister Dennis Wallace live to the west. My dad had pointed out their house to me once before. He'd said they were a couple of bachelor Indian brothers, even if their names don't sound like it.

Aunt Izzy says old Tom Sawyer was just showing his ignorance when he called his enemy "Injun Joe." We should not call them "Indians" because, before old Columbus told them, they'd never even heard of

India. But Columbus was completely lost, so I doubt if they believed him anyway.

I think they should be called something like "Leaping Eugene," and "He Who Eats Wild Onions Dennis," because that would sound more Indianish. Aunt Izzy says they should be called "Indigenous," or "Aborigines." An aborigine is just a wild person who got there first.

I guess I'll call them "Aborigine Eugene" and "Indigenous Dennis," because that should please Aunt Izzy and it would look swell on the front page of *The Buffalo County Trans-Weekly Disciplinarian*—in case worse came to even worse:

"Innocent settlers killed and massacred by the evil and malcontented Aborigine Eugene and Indigenous Dennis"

Any time you see a word that starts with "mal" you just as well figure it's going to be bad, because it is. Like I said, I know more "M" words than any others because my dog, Virgil, peed on the "M" section. So the "M" pages tend to bunch up and smell bad. For some reason the "Ns" and the "Os," got missed, but the "Ps" got a little damp and always open to "potato bug." I already know all I want about potato bugs because my dad makes me pick them off the vines. He pays me a penny apiece and says I must save my money for a rainy day, but I would rather spend it and hope for a slight sprinkle.

By breakfast time, Aunt Izzy had gotten over her ozone snit and was back to normal—if she had one. I never mentioned the Jesse James Hideout and Coal Mine. Instead, I asked her would it be all right if I sat in the driver's seat of the Pierce Arrow.

She said, "Of course it would be all right," and

she was sorry the horn wouldn't blow because the battery had been dead for years.

I figured that was some constellation for Uncle Willard because he wouldn't be the only one who was dead.

I dried the dishes again and Aunt Izzy reckoned she should do a little work in the garden. She asked me did I know how to pick potato bugs, and I told her I just guessed I *did*. I told her my dad paid me two pennies per bug—which was not exactly the truth, but I could have told her a nickel—and that I planned to save my bug money for Business College.

So, when we went outside, she got me a can and poured some coal oil in it to put the bugs in. Potato bugs don't like coal oil at all. But, like Aunt Izzy says, "We didn't exactly invite them over for lunch, did we?"

Whether those potato bugs liked that coal oil or not, some of them did show "personality." I can't really tell you what "personality" is, but if you want to see it, put a few potato bugs into a can of coal oil. Some of them will scramble like mad to get out, and some will just sink right to the bottom like it was all the same to them. But there's always one who will climb up on the back of another one, and he is the one with the most personality. And he has probably been to Business College.

Aunt Izzy wore a big, floppy straw hat because she said she didn't want to look like a prune when she got old. It was too late, but it didn't behoove me to say so.

We worked in that potato patch until the sun started getting hot, and Aunt Izzy decided we had done enough for today. She said, "Just pour those old bugs out and count them, and I'll pay you."

I said, "Oh, no, Ma'am, I couldn't take any money for helping."

"Well that's very nice of you, Jeffie!" She looked surprised enough to blister. But I was even more surprised.

I told her that lots of times I picked bugs for free for Mose Washington, and she said, "What in the world is a 'Mose Washington?'"

I told her Mose was my friend and he was a Negro. I told her we had a pair of Negroes right there in Epic. And I told her that Mose had a wooden leg and a Voodoo Queen, named "Mew," for a wife.

Aunt Izzy started over to the bench under the piss elm tree, so I set the can of potato bugs on a rock so they could get a little sun, and followed her. We sat there in the piss elm shade and Aunt Izzy said, "Tell me about these friends of yours, Jeffie."

"Well, like I said, Mose has a wooden leg because of an alligator and now he has a new one because the old one kept getting an abscess in its knot hole and the only thing that would stop it from hurting was a jug of Mr. Rasmusson's 'Null and Void.' So Mew made him build a new leg that wouldn't abscess. He made it out of a piece of maple, which was a mistake because maple is a pretty white wood. So some of the people there in Epic said he was getting 'uppity' and trying to pass himself off as part white. They said it just wasn't right, and probably illegal, for a black fellow to have a white leg. So, finally, Mose just painted that leg black, and everybody was happy. Well...it's not like they invited him to join the Knights of Columbus or the Blue Lodge, but they started treating him regular again.

"The best thing about Mose is, he doesn't treat me like a kid. Whenever I want to know the truth about something, I ask Mose, because he don't lie."

Aunt Izzy pulled an understanding grin, and said,

"Mose sounds like quite a friend. Now, I can't wait to hear about that Voodoo Queen!"

"Well, Mew is tall and skinny. I guess she's about a Mose-and-a-half tall, and she never says she's a Voodoo Queen. It's just sort of something you know. She always has a lot of feathers and seashells around, and she can heal anybody of anything. Unless, I guess, you have an abscess in your knot hole."

Aunt Izzy grinned and said that, so far, the good Lord had spared her from that indignity.

Aunt Izzy admitted that I was quite a talker when I got started. The truth of it was, with all the talking I had done, I still hadn't used my new daily word. She had forgotten all about teaching me the spelling and exact meaning of "Lollapaluski," so I just went ahead and found a new word on my own.

"Whither," got randomed because I was trying to avoid "M" words because it would likely just be "motley" again, and I'm sick of motleys.

Anyway, "whither" is not a word a fellow can drop just anywhere in a conversation. A whither is sort of when you know you are going somewhere, but you don't know where. I think it's a word you use when you're talking Bible or Shakespeare. Maybe like old Romeo would say, "Whither are you going with them dang chickens, Juliet?"

Well, Aunt Izzy said she'd like to sit and visit all day, but thought she would lie down for a while because she couldn't take the sun like she used to. I told her I'd be down at the barn looking at the Pierce Arrow, and she said now she was glad she'd kept that old Breezer.

It wasn't a question of "whithering" it, either. I was, for sure, going to the barn and I was, for sure, going to walk right past that Pierce Arrow and see some French ladies.

5

I eschewed the longer path to the barn and took a short cut. Now, that's the second time I've used that word since it randomed out as my word for the day. My mom told me I should "try some of that spinach," and I told her, "Spinach is a food I would eschew."

My dad said, "*Gesundheit.*"

My mom said, "How many times have I told you to cover your mouth when you sneeze?"

It is very difficult to learn an education in my family.

Anyway, I cut through the weeds, and you ought to have seen all the grasshoppers! Aunt Izzy said it was a bad year for the grasshoppers. She'd thought they were bad in the Hoover administration, but Franklin D. Roosevelt wasn't doing a bit better. She'd said "Politicians are all alike. They spend their four years in office debating about whether to put mayonnaise or mustard on the Sandwich Islands, and never do a thing about the goddamn grasshoppers."

That just shows how adults think. Looked to me like it was a *good* year for grasshoppers. Any way you figure it, there was a plethora of grasshoppers involved in that eschewing.

Besides being near grasshoppered to death on the way to the barn, I also got my ankle clutched by a devil's claw weed. I'll tell you, it just made me wonder if French ladies were worth getting grass-hoppered and devil's-clawed-on-the-ankle for.

I'll swear that old gas mask winked at me when I opened the lid of the trove. But I wasn't in any mood to make pleasantries with a stupid gas mask. I went straight for the treasure. I lined those French ladies up on the inside edge of the top of the trove and in-dulged my predilection.

A "predilection" is something a fellow is in favor of, and I happened to be in favor of French ladies.

Anyway, I squatted down amongst the straw and the bird poop and got comfortable because it takes a long time to look at naked French ladies. But, you know what I found out? French ladies look right back at you! Oh, they smile at you, and some even wink—but they're looking. And then I noticed that even their belly buttons were staring at me. But *they* weren't winking.

And then I saw that one of those French ladies was kind of looking over my shoulder and then the one down on the end was looking over my shoulder, and the little hairs on the back of my neck started grizzling right up.

Well, I'm not a fool—or maybe I am. I should have remembered that anytime you have a treasure trove, you leave a ghost or a skeleton around to guard it.

I didn't see him, but I felt him there. He was right behind me: Great Uncle dead Willard. His bony hands were reaching out to grab my innocent ears and shake me to death for looking at his personal naked French ladies. He was there, in his army coat and his dead-skull gas mask.

I started gathering up those pictures, as fast as I could, but neat and careful. And while I did I was hollering, "Dear Heavenly Father, please bless this food to our nourishment that we may endeavor..." I tucked those French ladies back in their little cardboard trove—gentle, as if I were their French momma—and slammed the lid.

I couldn't back up to get away. Great Uncle dead Willard was right behind me breathing his dead-spinach breath down my neck. I dodged sideways and made for the barn door.

I didn't even glance at the Pierce Arrow as I flew past it. I knew if I did, it would start honking at me, especially since it had a dead battery.

If there was a reasonable reason to stop running before I reached the back door of the house it did not occur to me. Before I collapsed on the step, I checked for the followence of a bony ghost. He was gone.

Well, I sat there on that old stone step until I'd cooled off some and was able to sort of smile at the whole happening. I hadn't really been scared. I expect old Tom Sawyer would have wet his pants, and the Radio Boys would have been waving their arms hollering, "Help, Mom! S.O.S., S.O.S.!"

The truth of the matter is, I'm just one of those boys who doesn't need all day to look at a few pictures.

Aunt Izzy was awake from her nap when I went inside. She was puttering around the kitchen, running her fingers through her hair. "I swear, Jeffie, I can't stand this long hair one minute longer. Tomorrow—off it comes! I would have had it cut on Monday, but I knew Little Willard was bringing you, and he likes to see me looking like an old maid school marm."

She held up an old magazine and said, "This is how I used to look, and this is how I am going to look tomorrow. Do you know who this is?"

The lady in the photograph was pure beautiful, even though she had clothes on.

"Wow!" I blurted, "She's French!"

Aunt Izzy gave me a queer look. "French?" she said, "Now, why would you think that?"

"Um, some women are," I suggested weakly. Aunt Izzy didn't see me turn red all over.

"No, Ma'am," I added, looking again at the photo, "I guess I don't know her."

"Well, this is Louise Brooks, and this time tomorrow, I'll look just like her!"

The lady's haircut made it look like she was wearing a football helmet. It was an eye-opening lesson for me. Women seem to be more beautiful if they are wearing football helmets.

Aunt Izzy stepped over to the icebox to chip some ice for our drinks: Coffin varnish for herself, and grape Kool-Aid for me. She joined me at the kitchen table, sighing and smiling into her drink. Now, I expect I like a good, cold Kool-Aid as well as the next fellow, but I can't say I've ever smiled at it like an old friend.

We sat at the kitchen table and she lifted her long hair with both hands, sort of fanned her neck with it, and said, "Dang, I'll be glad to get rid of this hot hair." She sounded almost angry. Still and all, another one of her "little drinky poos" put the smile back on her lips.

Finally I screwed up my courage and said, "Aunt Izzy, do you believe in ghosts?"

She wrinkled up her forehead in thought, so I knew she was going to tell me the truth. "Well, Jeffie, I suppose I do, maybe a little bit. Do you believe in ghosts?"

"Naw," I said, "I don't think so. But Pinky Smail claims he saw one at the top of his stairs once. He said it was wearing a derby hat, so I think he was lying. He usually does."

Aunt Izzy refilled her glass and sat back down, still wearing her thinking frown. "Now, Jeffie, maybe we shouldn't be too judgmental about ghosts. Maybe this old ghost just loved derby hats and wore one all his life. Maybe he wouldn't be caught dead without one." When she realized what she'd said, she spluttered her drink out all over the table laughing. "No disrespect intended, Mr. Ghost!" She wiped off the table with a dishrag, and said, "By gosh, if I'm ever a ghost I'm going to wear a derby! That'll just be the cat's pajamas!"

I expect there's not a fellow in the world that could picture Aunt Izzy in a derby hat, wearing a cat's pajamas, and not laugh. I laughed too.

"But seriously, Jeffie, a lot of people *do* believe in ghosts. Take my neighbor, Eugene, for instance, he sure believes in them. He's one of the two brothers you call 'Indians.'"

"Yes, ma'am," I admitted, "but that was before I learned they were really "Indigenous Aborigines."

Aunt Izzy took a close look up at the ceiling, and said, "Oh, Lord."

It was the first time I'd ever noticed her saying grace before taking a drink, and I knew my dad would be happy to know she was setting a good example for me.

Well here I am, rattling on and on about Aunt Izzy's drinking; I'll have you thinking she was always "blotto" or "splifficated," and that's just not the case at all. It's more like she has a proclivity in the shape of drinky poos.

A "proclivity" is a natural inclination toward drinky poos.

Anyway, like I was saying, Aunt Izzy was *never* what you call "drunk"—not even close to it. What she was was grinfully happy.

"So tell me about Aborigine Eugene's ghosts," I begged.

"Well, now, Eugene is a cagey old man but he does have some weird ways. He believes there's a spirit in everything: stones, trees, fence posts, most likely even apples. But the only one that scares him is Jesse James' spirit that he claims hangs out in the mine."

"Holy cow! Has he really seen it—or him? Was he wearing a derby hat?"

"I don't think he really saw it," Aunt Izzy said, "I think he just smelled the cookies baking."

That was when I started thinking that poor old Aunt Izzy'd had one proclivity too many.

She considered me with a long look. Like she wanted to be sure I wasn't the kind of boy who would steal the family silver or pee out the back door. Then she seemed to kind of soften and said, "Now, Jeffie, I know I was a little short with you last night, and I'm sorry. But what I'm about to tell you is a secret. I've never before told a soul, and you must not either, especially not your dad, Little Willard. You see, I've always had sort of a soft spot in my heart for Jesse James. Maybe it's because I was born on his birthday, September fifth, and right here at one of his hideouts. The truth is, Jesse James wasn't as bad as folks like to make out.

"After the War of Northern Aggression and all that

foolishness was over, Jesse bought himself this little coal mine right here. It was just a scratch-in-the-ground kind of place, but he was planning ahead to pursue a career in the bank and train robbery business. He knew he would need a lot of hideouts, and he figured to stock them all with a good supply of coal."

Aunt Izzy took a deep swig and looked at me like maybe I had not understood. "Well, hell," she said, "outlaws get cold, too, you know!

"Anyway, Jesse did right well with that mine. In fact, he was starting to think about abandoning his dreams of a life of crime. He was about to sign a contract with the Devil to supply the anthracite for the fires of Hell, but there was something about Jesse that the old Devil just didn't cotton to. So the Devil backed out.

"Well, sir, that just kind of put poor old Jesse down in the dumps. Seems like he lost all interest in his coal business.

"Now, here's something the history books won't tell you, and Jesse and I would appreciate it if you don't spread it around: there was nothing in the world Jesse would rather do than putter around the kitchen."

Somehow something had shifted. Now she seemed to be lumping herself and Jesse James together like they were gum-buddies. I kept my mouth shut, and she went on.

"So poor old Jesse was so dispirited he made himself a little kitchen kind of place there in the mine and set about making cookies. Lord knows there was enough coal for the oven.

"Sometimes folks would see him and his brother, Frank, riding along with bags across their saddles and think they were full of gold. Pshaw! They were nothing but bags of cookies. 'Train Robber cookies,' Jesse called them. His own secret recipe. They were always a great hit with those outlaws lollygagging around the campfires. And the truth was, you couldn't eat just one."

"Aunt Izzy," I said, "how come you know all those Jesse James secrets?"

She stared past me at a blank spot on the wall; her eyes showed a little wet. "Oh, I guess I just know them," she said. "Jesse and I don't keep secrets."

6

First thing next morning I randomed my word for the day: Ostrich!

See, my rule is to use my new word three times in a sentence to be sure I remember it. You have to know a lot of words if you plan to be a book writer, and I've been considering that kind of job as a lifetime pursuit.

I wonder, has anyone ever figured how to use "ostrich" three times in one day without sounding like a complete fool? Still and all, I'm also thinking I might rather be a "Matriarch" than a book writer. Aunt Izzy sure seems to enjoy being one, and I'm beginning to think a Matriarch can make up stories just as well as a book writer. But I have never heard her use the word "ostrich."

I made myself a mental note to never write a book about an ostrich, and re-randomed.

"Coniferous." A coniferous is a tree. So why don't they just say tree? I never read anything about Tom Sawyer climbing a stupid coniferous to look for Injun

Joe. I'm pretty sure he never saw an ostrich either. If he did, I doubt it was from the top of a coniferous. And he had the good sense not to mention it to Aunt Polly—she would have whaled him good. Aunt Polly never seemed like a person who would take much guff from a mythical bird or a coniferous, either.

I heard Aunt Izzy rattling around in the kitchen making breakfast, so my word for the day would just have to wait.

My first look in the kitchen told me I was no longer company. There was no bacon, no eggs and no biscuits. Instead, Aunt Izzy was pouring Grape Nuts into a pot of boiling water.

"You're boiling the Grape Nuts?" I bewildered.

Yeah, I know, it was a dumb question, but it really wasn't a question. It was more of an amazement.

"Well, of course," Aunt Izzy said, "raw Grape Nuts will kill you! I read in the *Capper's Weekly* a while back about a woman in Michigan...I think it was in Michigan...where a woman's three kids had diphtheria. She fed them raw Grape Nuts, and in less than a week they were all dead."

"But I always eat raw Grape Nuts!"

"Not at my house, you don't. I'm not going to have people saying I killed my great-nephew with diphtheria!"

It may be that boiled Grape Nuts could have been worse, but then, I've never had diphtheria.

We finished breakfast without talking much. Mostly Aunt Izzy just stared at me. "I can't understand how you can still be alive. Don't your parents subscribe to *Capper's Weekly?*"

Twenty minutes later we were whizzing down the highway in Aunt Izzy's Model A Ford on our way to Armageddon. The windshield was open and her long hair was flying. She laid out her plan for the day:

"First of all, I'll get this hair whacked off. You can either wait in the beauty parlor for me or hang around outside and watch our pretty Armageddon girls."

"I don't want to watch no darn girls," I told her. I know I turned red because she laughed and winked at me. "You're not fooling me, Mr. Jefferson Davis Johnson."

I guess I'll never know how moms and women do it, but somehow Aunt Izzy knew I'd been looking at French ladies, and also wondering what the next-door Potts girls looked like.

One look through that beauty parlor window and I knew I wasn't going in. There were four women sitting in beauty parlor chairs with about a hundred wires attached to their heads. I'd seen enough picture shows to know that any time now a priest would walk in and give them their extreme function. Then the warden would throw the switch and the lights would dim and they'd be fried.

I don't mind telling you, I was all of a sudden scared. If Aunt Izzy went in there and got fried, I would be a hopeless orphan with two Indians living on one side of me and two girls named Potts on the other. If ever I was sorry for burning down the dang outhouse, it was then.

Aunt Izzy gave me a quick squeeze and said I was a sweet boy—not wanting her to get fried and all. She said she'd watch them suckers like a hawk, and if they tried to fry her, old Jesse James would come in and shoot their butts off. Well, I wasn't going to count much on a fellow who'd been dead for fifty years! The best I could hope for was that old Hopalong Cassidy would occur.

When the door clicked shut behind her, I was sure she had forgiven me for not dying of diphtheria back when I was a heathen eating my Grape Nuts raw. I asked God to please protect Aunt Izzy from being fried and bless this food for the nourishment of our souls and bodies.

Two doors down the street I found the ultimate, end-of-the-world treasure trove. It was what they call a "pawnshop," and you'd have to see it to believe it. I truly believe the King of England himself would have just wet his pants in envy. Right there in the window—there were accordions and banjos and wristwatches and revolvers and, if you can name it, I expect there were at least three of them.

I didn't take a step further. I just stood and stared at all those glories. I knew I would never in a million years become a book writer or even a Matriarch. I would be a pawn guy, and there was even a piece of cardboard with juice harps on it.

And that's where Aunt Izzy found me, if it was Aunt Izzy; it was hard to tell. It mostly was, I guess. And her hair really *did* look like that French lady, Louise Brooks.

She made a complete turnaround and said, "How do you like it?"

Out of nowhere I remembered that old movie star, Morees Chevrolet. His smooth style came to my rescue. I bowed and repeated what I hoped I'd heard him say in French, *"Apres vous, Mamzell."*

And I guess I was close enough because she said, "Come on, we'll go over to F.W. Woolworth's and have some chop suey."

We found seats at the lunch counter, and Aunt Izzy told me F.W. Woolworth's made the best chop suey in the world. I admitted to the fact that I hope they boiled it good, because that's the way we always had it at home.

Aunt Izzy said I was a real lollypaluski, and she was sure glad I had come for a visit. So was I.

By and by the waitress brought our bowls. "Here's your chop suey, Miss Louise Brooks," she giggled, "and one for your handsome young beau."

If you have ever wondered why the Chinese people have their eyes all squinted up, it's because of chop suey. Chop suey is not a thing you want to look at too closely. Not if you plan to eat it.

Aunt Izzy told me to "dig in," so I did. It crossed my mind that I would sure have a few things to tell old Pinky Smail and Purdy Grundy when I got back home. What with boiled Grape Nuts for breakfast, and chop suey for lunch, I knew I was becoming a "Man of the World."

Anyway, when I started to pour the ketchup on, Aunt Izzy stopped me. She said the Chinese were very set in their traditional ways, and it would probably take another thousand years before they learned to put ketchup on their chop suey.

Now, taken day in and day out, chop suey is a food I can take or I can leave alone, but Aunt Izzy was right. I had never had better. I guess if those starving children in China had good old F.W. Woolworth make their chop suey they wouldn't complain so much.

On the way home, what with a haircut and a bowl of chop suey, Aunt Izzy was in a good mood. First thing I knew she was belting out "I Wish I Could Shimmy Like My Sister Kate." A "belt out" is what you do when you *really* want to sing "I Wish I Could Shimmy Like My Sister Kate."

So down the highway we rolled. Aunt Izzy singing and shimmying—probably better than most people could shimmy in the driver's seat of a Model A Ford at fifty-five miles an hour.

By the time she got to the part of the song that went, "like a plate full of jelly," Aunt Izzy was moving her butt in such a spectacular manner that she knocked the gear shift thing into neutral.

"Copacetic!" I shouted, "You didn't even use the clutch!"

"Damn right, Kiddo," she hollered, "They don't call me 'clutch butt' for nothing!" We rolled to a stop laughing.

By the time we got home, Aunt Izzy had declared herself ready for a party.

"Is it your birthday?" I asked, surprised.

"Oh, my no," she said. "Jesse and I celebrate our birthdays on September 5. I'm just talking about a *party* party."

Well, sir, that was some constellation for me. I wasn't about to go to any dang party where Jesse James' ghost might show up. We spent about an hour and a half listening to the Victrola until I knew all the words to "Sister Kate" backwards and forwards. Aunt Izzy dug out a flat straw hat she called a "skimmer." It had belonged to Great Uncle dead Willard, and was about twelve times too big for me, but she stuffed it full of newspaper until it sort of fit. "I'll call Dennis and see if he wants to party tonight," she said. "Then maybe we should rest awhile."

The goings-on of the day had taken a toll on Aunt Izzy. A "toll" is about the same as a "troll" because they both take something from you. Except a troll has legs and always wants your first-born child. If you look at it that way, I guess she was lucky it was a toll because she didn't have a first-born or any other borns.

Anyway, I went to my bedroom like Aunt Izzy wanted, but I really wasn't sleepy. The first thing I saw was my dictionary, and I was ashamed to face it. I knew I had been a piker about the words "ostrich" and "coniferous." Facing the hard facts, I knew old

Mark Twain would never have left those words lying there unused. No, sir, if he had to, he would have written about Huck chopping down a coniferous to build a raft. And he would have had him free an ostrich instead of Nigger Jim, and off they'd go. Right down that old Mississippi River they'd go: a boy and his runaway ostrich friend, on their good old coniferous. Nobody would ever think a thing about it.

Aunt Izzy fixed us some peanut butter sandwiches for supper so as not to have a big mess to clean up. She poured a little fancy glass of wine for herself. I expect, as with so many other edibles, some wines go better with peanut butter sandwiches than others.

The parlor was spick and span, as it always was, but we drug the little throw rugs into the dining room. Aunt Izzy said she didn't want us tripping and breaking our necks while dancing. Using a broom to enforce her encouragement, she herded the thousands of Rudolphs out the back door.

Aunt Izzy emptied the contents of a Mason jar into a cut glass decanter, and placed it and some glasses on the table. With her usual thoughtfulness, she'd made a pitcher of grape Kool-Aid for me.

She was all aflutter with excitement, and I'll confess, I was a little nervous too. Whether she would admit it or not, Dennis was an Indian. And, yes, Indians do dance: they Rain Dance, they Scalp Dance and they War Dance.

And maybe I was wishing I had been sent to Nebraska for my penal punishment vacation.

I sat, waiting, in the parlor. Aunt Izzy was back in her bedroom adding "a few finishing touches." My legs were crossed like that fellow in the magazines who wants everyone to notice his elegant Florsheim shoes.

As a gesture of good will to my first adult party, I had, on my own recognizance, mixed a little of Aunt Izzy's giggle water into my Kool-Aid. "Heckfire," I thought, "I'm a grown up."

After a while I thought, "Hellfire yes, I'm a grown up!"

So I sat there, a grown up adult—practically wearing Florsheim shoes—waiting for that Indian: considering. He just better not try any of that massacre crap around here, I thought. I'll give him a *knuckle* sandwich and let him decide what wine he wants with *that*. I took another little drinky poo to seal the deal.

Still and all, Dennis was our guest and I knew I must be polite. When the knock on the door finally came, I opened the door and offered my hand.

"Welcome, Indigenous Dennis!" I cried, "I'm Jefferson Davis Johnson. Seen any ostriches today?"

7

Old Indigenous Dennis stood there, staring at me, like he'd never before seen a fellow almost wearing Florsheim shoes.

"Come on in and we'll get splifficated," I invited.

I'd just as well tell you right off, as an Indian, old Indigenous Dennis was a flat disappointment. Being a good Presbyterian and all, I wouldn't say this to his face, but Indigenous Dennis would *never* be the one to put either the "pow!" or the "wow!" in powwow.

He wore neither war bonnet nor war paint, neither medicine bag nor moccasins; carried neither tomahawk nor a stupid tom tom.

Yeah, I know, nobody promised me a warpath Indian, but you'd think even an Indigenous would show a little pride.

As a sheik, I guess he could pass. He wore a flat skimmer hat, and he had wingtip shoes with the wingtips painted white. He also sported a bamboo walking stick. But when a fellow is hoping for a bloody tomahawk, a bamboo walking stick seemed mighty wimpy.

Now, in all fairness to those of the Indigenous persuasion, I'll admit I might not have been what he expected either. But I stepped aside, grinning, and gave my glass of Kool-Aid and giggle water a sophisticated little swirl.

Just then Aunt Izzy came bouncing into the room and old Dennis had something more interesting to look at than me.

"Hail, Hail, the gang's all here," she squealed.

She was pure dynamite!

Any plans old Indigenous might have had for scalping the settlers and burning the cabin were plainly forgotten.

Aunt Izzy struck a pose, and I'll tell you what, I figured I'd "been around the block a few times," as the fellow says, and if ever I'd seen a French lady, it was her.

She stood with her left knee bent, and her right hip pushed out 'til it looked painful. In her right hand she held a cigarette in her ivory holder, and the smoke rolled out her nose like a St. George dragon.

Her "Louise Brooks" haircut sported a huge butterfly that had first planned to be a peacock's feather, but had found a better calling. Now... that dress of hers was all made of beads: purple-changing-color-beads, from top to bottom. But her knees were discreetly hidden by a lampshade kind of fringe contraption. A "discreet" is when you know a woman probably has knees, but you're not going to find out from her.

Indigenous Dennis's eyes bulged out and I expect mine did, too. But he also grinned a grin that told the world he knew something that others could only wish they knew.

The first words out of his mouth were, "Why, Izzy, you look stunning." That surprised me, because Indians, even if they're only Indigenouses, usually just say, "Ugh!" But saying "Ugh" would have likely been a bad mistake.

Aunt Izzy blushed. "Okay, you Oliver Twisters, who's first in line for a little drinky poo-avous?" Aunt Izzy demanded.

I was hoping old Indigenous Dennis would talk some Indian, and he did. "Woo Woo, that's me-avous for a drinky poo!" he whooped.

When they'd fixed their drinks and turned to wind up the Victrola, I devised myself a little more Kool-Aid, splashed in some more poo-avous—and knew I was the handsomest, most smoldering sheik in Buffalo County, Kansas.

A band started playing inside the Victrola, and Ethel Waters began loudly explaining that she was getting sick and tired of telling people to shake that thing. But she did keep telling them. Aunt Izzy and Indigenous Dennis did their best to please her. Waving their hands and humping their shoulders, shaking—like "jelly on a plate."

When the music ended, Aunt Izzy gave me a big wink, and one last, bone-rattling shake of what I had come to believe was "that thing."

Puffing like a danged old steam engine, Aunt Izzy flopped the record over and gave the crank a few more turns. It was Ethel Waters again, and this time she was singing "No Man's Mamma."

Now as far as I was concerned, "No Man's Mamma" couldn't hold a candle to "Shake That Thing." It was just a song about how a judge signed some papers so's Ethel could sell one of her beds and go off, flittering and fluttering around. Still and all, adults get amused about strange things, and if they like to sing about going into the used furniture business, it's all right with me.

Well, it was just pretty easy to see that my presence would not be required in the near future, so I kind'a shook my thing over to the end table and fixed myself another one of what had become my favorite drink.

When the music stopped, the two dancers sort of collapsed onto the sofa and found their drinks. Aunt Izzy picked up a funeral home fan and flat put it to work. It was one of those fans with a picture of Jesus on it, and when she stopped fanning for a minute, old Jesus was looking right straight at me.

Now, it's a funny thing...I mean, I knew it was just a picture...but, still and all, it made me squirm. I eased my drink down beside my chair as if it weren't anything but a nonchalant, and gave Jesus a little grin. With any luck at all, He might think it was just Kool-Aid.

When Aunt Izzy got her breath back, she started showing me how to work the player piano. She showed me how to install the paper rolls, so's not to tear them, then how to work the levers and pump the peddles. When the music came out it was just grand, and you would have bet your last dollar Aunt Izzy was doing the playing herself.

She sat me on the piano bench and laid three Jelly Roll Morton rolls atop the piano: "The Black Bottom Stomp," "The Stratford Hunch" and "The Turtle Twist."

She grabbed old Indigenous by the hand and pulled him to his feet.

"Pump away, Mr. Jelly Roll Johnson," she said. "We're going to 'cut a rug'!"

So I pumped away and they danced and laughed. Finally, Aunt Izzy declared an intermission and, while she brought some sandwiches from the kitchen, Indigenous Dennis chipped more ice from the big block in the icebox for our drinks.

"And now it's time for the big surprise!" Aunt Izzy announced. She disappeared to her bedroom and came back brandishing a ukulele. It was a surprise for me, all right. She adjusted my skimmer to a cocky angle over my left eye, and handed me Indigenous's bamboo walking stick.

She raised her hand for attention and old Indigenous started clapping like you might expect if she was riding a buffalo. But she wasn't. She just started talking: "Ladies and gentlemen, tonight we are happy to bring for your listening pleasure, the famous and fabulous Johnson and Johnson team. And so... straight from the stages of New York City... here they are!"

Aunt Izzy kind of elbowed me, winked, and whispered, "Sister Kate."

When she started thrumping that old ukulele I guess you could say I was amazed. Then she started singing and, of course, so did I.

Now you might think I would be feeling pretty silly, but that wasn't the case. Because, see, I had lost my "inhibitions." Inhibitions are what you lose just before you make a plum fool of yourself. But I wasn't worried.

We sang and we shimmied and we shimmied and sang. Aunt Izzy's fingers were flying all over that ukulele 'til I just wished I could have sat down and watched. Old Indigenous looked about to collapse from laughing.

When our song ended the applause was loud, but didn't last long. The applauder was showing a few signs of wear.

And, to tell the truth, my old battery seemed to

be running down too. What with the singing, piano playing, smoky air and my new invention, the Kool-Aid Delight, I was starting to droop.

Aunt Izzy said she reckoned old "Vicky, the Victrola" had cooled off, so they wound it up and went back to dancing.

I laid a few piano roll boxes out on the floor and sat beside them to sort them out, and that's where I was when they woke me—sleeping—right between Rudy Valee and Ethel Waters.

8

I woke next morning with the firm belief that if, as some folks say, the world is going to end soon—this would be a dang good day for it.

In point of fact, as the fellow says, I prayed to Jesus for it to happen.

My dad prays directly to God. He says it's always best to do business with the top man. My dad went to Business College so he also knows God is a Republican.

Understand now, my dad doesn't put Jesus down, not in any way shape or form. It's just that ever since He chased those moneychangers out of the Temple, my dad's not too sure He has the best interests of the banking business at heart.

Anyway, I felt the worst kind of awful. I hadn't fooled that funeral-parlor-fan-picture of Jesus about my Kool-Aid, not for a minute. I expect it was my stupid grin that did it, and I learned my lesson: don't grin at Jesus!

No way in the world was I about to let Aunt Izzy

know I was hung over. Maybe I wasn't. Maybe I was lucky and just had a brain tumor and diphtheria.

My dad sometimes pointed out a drunk to me. "Just look at him," he'd say. "A disgrace to himself and his whole family! Picking up cigar butts from the gutter! He'll end up lying in the gutter himself."

Well, now, from my point of view, a good, comfortable gutter didn't sound too bad just then. It would likely beat sitting down to a bowl of boiled Grape Nuts all hollow.

Aunt Izzy wasn't fooled, no way. "Good morning, sleepyhead. Wow! You don't look so good." She fiddled a moment at the kitchen cabinet and handed me a glass of spiked tomato juice.

"Don't worry, you'll live. I've been there myself a few times. All you need is a little of the hair of the dog that bit you."

If she'd dropped a dang dog hair in my tomato juice I knew I'd puke. I started to tell her about my brain tumor and diphtheria but, instead, I puked anyway.

Well, this is a hard thing to admit, but I felt so rotten about puking on Aunt Izzy's kitchen floor that I started crying like a baby. I sat there and, what with the tears, the dog hairs and the thought of boiled Grape Nuts, I puked again.

Aunt Izzy didn't get mad at all. She pulled my head up against her hipbone and said, "It's okay, Jeffie." I knew right then I'd love her forever.

She did make me drink all the spiked tomato juice though, and if there were any dog hairs in it I didn't find them.

"Let's get you into the parlor and onto the couch for awhile." I didn't argue. I'll tell you though, that old parlor did not look as jolly as it had last night. I flat averted my eyes from the dang Victrola and the piano.

An "eye avert" is when you know you'll puke again if you look at a piano.

Anyway, Aunt Izzy was just as understanding as a human can be. "You had a little too much bacchanalia last night," she explained.

"Well, I'll never do it again," I promised. "I guess I got the wrong bottle, I thought I had the giggle water."

I woke to the jangling of the telephone, one short, two longs, one short. That was Aunt Izzy's ring.

It was also the letter "P" in the Morse code. I knew that because, before I decided to be a book writer or maybe a Matriarch, I was learning to be a telegraph guy like old Dunk Parmley back home in Epic. Still and all, I didn't want to be *just* like old Dunk. See, his false teeth clicked and clacked just like the telegraph machine and it confused him something awful. For instance, you might get a telegram telling you that your tractor was invited to Aunt Minnie's birthday party when you didn't even have a tractor with an Aunt Minnie.

Anyway, Aunt Izzy came in saying, "That'll be Mrs. Potts." And it was. Seemed to me as if maybe Aunt Izzy must be psychic—or maybe I mean physic, like a Carter's Little Liver Pill. I can't keep those words straight, so you better check before you take one.

"Yes, Ma'am, that'll be fine," she told Mrs. Potts and hung up.

"That snoopy old biddy! She says she wants to borrow a cup of sugar, but I know what she really wants. She's had her spyglass out again and knows I have company. She won't be able to sleep until she finds out who it is."

Thank goodness the nap made me feel better, but I still wasn't hungry. Aunt Izzy said I just had time to get dressed and brush my hair.

When the knock came I was ready. It was Mrs. Potts and her two daughters, Lucille and Pauline.

I guess they looked pretty much like you'd expect a family of Potts to look. And considering how poor I was feeling a couple of hours ago, the sight of the Potts' somehow made me feel downright chipper.

The mama Pott made me want to sing "I'm a little tea pot short and stout" and, if I'd really been singing, I'd have added, "…pick me up, and throw me out."

I wondered if she ever called the kettle black.

As for the thirteen-year old daughter, Lucille, she was tall and skinny, except for her butt. In my wicked mind I was seeing a future boy friend trying to write a love poem and searching for a rhyme for "vinegar cruet."

On the other hand, the younger sister, Pauline was sort of cute; kind of like what Aunt Izzy called a "demitasse." Her hair was so black it was sometimes a little purplish; her eyes were brown and ornery. I figured she might be part Aborigine or Indigenous— at least her head part.

Turned out she was two months older than I was, and if she'd been a boy I might have liked her. Still and all, not a one of those three Potts would ever be a French lady.

Aunt Izzy chipped some ice off the block in the icebox and served us all glasses of tea. We sat around the table and she explained we'd had company last night, and the parlor was "simply a mess."

"The tea is already sugared," she said.

Mrs. Potts allowed as how she "could not stomach" tea without sugar, and we settled in to get acquainted.

The mama Pott sat straight across from Aunt Izzy, and Lucille sat at the end-place like she was the almighty ruler of the world. Pauline sat next to me.

First thing I knew, that little whelp kicked me in the ankle. That was all right because we were just getting acquainted. But then, pretty soon, she kicked me in the ankle again. And that was what they call "presumptuous," because how did she know so soon that she didn't like me?

After a while Aunt Izzy suggested I take the girls outside and show them around the place. Old Lucille said she'd stay inside because she didn't want the sun to burn her *delicate skin.* Frankly, I figured she was more concerned in making sure the adults held their pinky fingers just *so* as they drank their tea than she was about her precious hide.

Pauline and I took the hint and went out the door. You can be dang sure I was keeping my eye on her kicking foot too.

"What do you want to do?" I asked, planning to be the perfect host—if only to keep from being kicked.

"You sure got funny ears!" she explained.

"Well, for such a runty kid, you got a big mouth," I told her. We started walking along, through the dust, not really going much of anywhere.

"You want to see Jesse James's old hideout?" I suggested.

"I guess so. It'd be better than standing around looking at your funny ears. Maybe we can find his hidden treasure." So we kept walking for a while and finally she asked, "Just how much farther do we have to walk to this old Jesse James thing?"

"I don't really know. I've never been there."

Pauline stopped dead and jammed her fists on her hipbones.

"You don't *know?* You've never been there? You are completely D-U-M-B—*dumb!*

"You got beans in your ears? I've never been there! And I'm not dumb. Aunt Izzy says the mine's dangerous. She told me to keep away from that place. Anyway, it's haunted."

"Well, I'm not afraid of any stupid ghosts!" she said. Maybe she wasn't, but for whatever reason, she got awful serious and thoughtful. And when we started walking again she walked mighty slow.

"There's no such thing as ghosts," she went on.

"Well then, Miss Not Afraid, how do you explain the smell of baking cookies?" I could see I had her there. For a girl with such a big mouth, she didn't have an answer for that. She stopped walking and decided she had a rock in her shoe.

She plopped herself down in the weeds and pulled off her shoe; if there was a rock there, it was a mighty little one. But she carried on like her foot would have to be amputated, and announced she couldn't walk anymore.

Like any girl, she could change the subject faster than you could blink. Likely, she had suddenly become just bored to death with ghosts.

"Do you know how to smoke?" she asked.

"Well, of course I do," I replied, "What a dumb question. How else would our privy have got burned down?" I knew I was on a roll. She wasn't so dang smart after all.

"Can you cuss?"

"Of course I can cuss. I'm a boy, aren't I? But I don't do it. I'm Presbyterian. My whole family is."

My quick answer didn't work that time, and she came right back at me. "I bet I know more cuss words than you!" she bragged.

"That's a plain lie," I told her, "Girls don't cuss."

Well, sir, she hopped up, one shoe on and one shoe off, looked me in the eye and flat told me, "Bull hockey!" And on she went, like a train afire, "Fart! Titty! Pissant!"

If ever I was nonplused, it was right then. I must have gone red all over, but she didn't let up. She leaned right up to one of those ears she had found so humorous, and whispered, "sumbich."

Then she gave me a kiss on the cheek and took off like she'd never had a sore foot in her life.

You can bet I didn't even take time to wipe off the germs. I was after her like a shot because, heckfire, I had to get ahead of her. If it looked like I was chasing her, my reputation as a Presbyterian would be shot to pieces.

I'll tell you, that little runt could run fast as a bullet! But I finally caught up to her, and for a while it was neck and neck. Then I passed her, and if I could stay ahead I would be safe.

When we reached the house, Mrs. Potts and old Vinegar Cruet Lucille were just saying their goodbyes. Neither one of them carried any sugar. I guess they forgot what they came for.

And then, right before my eyes, Pauline did a complete epitome. She nearly bowed and said, "Thank you for the tea and for a wonderful time, Miss Isabella." Then she turned to me and said, "And thank you, Jefferson Davis Johnson. It was lovely."

They walked off down the path and Aunt Izzy stayed by the screen door, so nobody heard me when I shook my head and mumbled, "Sumbich!"

9

My mom called next morning. I'd been outside and Aunt Izzy told me when I came in.

"Good news, Jeffie! I think you're off the hook about burning your privy. Your mom talked your dad into getting indoor plumbing. Lord, I don't know how she did it, as tight as he is with his money, but she finally found the gumption to stand up to him. Ida said she told him it was a disgrace when the wife of the town banker had to go to an Italian's house to 'visit Mrs. Jones,' and he ought to be ashamed of himself. I hate to say it, Jeffie, but your dad is the kind of man who'll buy a nickel cigar and then light it with a dollar bill just to show off. Anyhow, she convinced him it was the proper thing for a man of his standing to do, so he agreed."

"Wow," was the only thing I could think of to say. Aunt Izzy agreed.

She sat down with me at the table and considered her glass of giggle water. "You know, Jeffie, I've kind of been thinking of doing the same thing. I can afford it. I'm not rich, but your Great Uncle Willard left me better off than people know. There'd be no more going out to the backhouse on stormy nights, and no more getting stung on the butt by wasps. I could soak in the bathtub all day if I was so minded."

She tipped up her glass and swallowed her giggle water in one gulp.

"By God, and pardon my French," she said, "I'm going to do it!"

Well, sir, I was sorry to hear her say that. Probably been two hours since I'd even thought about those French ladies down in the barn, and now I'd learned that not only did they sit around wearing nothing but a fan and, maybe, a little French poodle, but they blasphemed as well.

Still and all, it's pretty hard to bear a grudge against a French lady.

Aunt Izzy brought the phone book to the table and started talking to herself and writing down numbers. "I'll need a contractor," she said. "One outfit to do the whole job."

I followed her to the parlor where the phone was, and listened as she cleared her throat and put on her best Matriarch voice. She told that fellow exactly what she wanted, where she wanted it, and when she wanted it—which was about *right now*—then hung up. I never saw anybody get things done like Aunt Izzy!

Then she suddenly raised her head and said, "Oh my gosh! I forgot to tell you. Your mom asked if I had you straightened up yet. I told her you were doing fine, but I thought it'd be better if you stayed about another week. I hope you don't mind, Jeffie, I should have asked you first."

I guess I grinned like a possum. "No, ma'am," I told her, "I don't mind at all."

Aunt Izzy set out to clean and straighten up the parlor, and I set out to ease the guilt I had for neglecting my dictionary. Careful, so's not to random another "M" word, I dug straight to the back. "Vernac-u-lar." A vernacular is the way people talk when there are no teachers around. I needed to use it three times today, but I knew I could do it. It'd be a whale of a lot easier than "ostrich!"

There was a patch of plowed ground between Aunt Izzy's place and where Aborigine Eugene and Indigenous Dennis lived. Aunt Izzy said those two brothers just didn't get around to planting anything this year. I figured they were off hunting buffalo. They should have spent their time planting, though, because there weren't any more buffaloes left in Kansas than there were ostriches.

I thought of that place as the "reservation," because that's where Indians go when there is a paucity of buffalo and ostriches and a plethora of white people. My teacher, Old Lady Whitfield, told us the natives had signed a treaty with the government, and the government would pay them money and hamburger for being Indians or Aborigines or Indigenouses, if they would just shut up and stay there on the reservation. And the government promised they could live on the reservation until the rocks turned to butter and the moon turned to "whey." But the Indians didn't know the government was a pack of liars, and they also didn't know whey from Shineola—or they would have planted something in that plowed field.

It looked like a first class place to hunt for arrowheads, and I'd started walking up and down with my eyes on the ground when old Indigenous Dennis hollered. He was carrying a small suitcase and looked raring to go somewhere.

"Good sunshine day, Paleface boy. You tellem Aunt me catchem Iron Horse. Go Tulsa. Getem teeth fixed. Tellem be back in two sleeps. Auf wiedersehen."

I was flat out embarrassed because I knew Aunt Izzy must have told him I'd been disappointed he wasn't more Indian. Still and all, I was sort of glad to see he hadn't forgotten all the Old Ways and could still talk Indian vernacular, even if he didn't likely know it was really Indigenous.

After a while I gave up. If there were any arrowheads on this reservation I couldn't find them. It must be pretty embarrassing for an Indian—not a speck of an arrowhead lying around. There'd be some mighty red-faced red-men I'm guessing. Ha! Red-faced red-men! If old Pauline thinks my ears are funny, just wait until she hears my jokes!

Back at home, I found Aunt Izzy busy cleaning out a spare first-floor bedroom for the new bathroom. She'd already moved out the chairs when I burst in with the news about Indigenous Dennis going to Tulsa to get his teeth fixed. "And he was talking all in Indian," I told her. "I could understand every word!"

Aunt Izzy cast me a doubtful look and I was about to inflict her that I was a truthful Presbyterian, but she gave me a weak smile and said, "That's very nice."

Together we pushed the chifforobe down the hall to another bedroom, and, last of all we tackled the bed. I'd never seen such a thing. There were no springs at all; just a bunch of ropes stretched around. Aunt Izzy said it was an "antique." An antique is something so old you have to use ropes to hold it together.

Well, I could see that bed was old. Even the dust

under it looked old. Likely it was a caveman bed or, maybe, Indigenous.

If Mrs. Whitfield wasn't lying, like I think she sometimes did, this could be an Indian bed. What probably happened was: the Indians never heard of bed springs until the crooked white men came. Then, when the white men started unloading them, hand over fist, from the Mayflower, one of the Indians happened to jump on one and it changed his life forever because it beat jumping on a rope bed all hollow.

I expect the government offered to trade a whole travois load of bed springs for New South Wales and throw in a broken shotgun. The Indians would have jumped at the chance. I guess that's how one of those now-useless rope beds ended up in Aunt Izzy's bedroom. But it couldn't stay if we were going to get indoor plumbing.

With the old bed cleared out and stored with the other junk, Aunt Izzy suggested I go chip some ice and pour us some tea while she stayed behind with the broom. I think Aunt Izzy was a little embarrassed that I'd seen all the dust but, heck, it was *antique* dust even if it wasn't roped up. Most likely, it was valuable and somebody probably collects antique dust. But it wasn't my place to mention it.

We were both hot and sweaty from all the work, but there was a cool breeze blowing through the house and Aunt Izzy was all smiles.

"You know what, Jeffie? Looks to me like that little Pauline's kinda taken a shine to you."

I didn't say anything. I just sort of blew some air out my lips in a *pfoo*.

"Well, it's nothing to be ashamed of, Jeffie. You're getting old enough to have a girlfriend."

I'll tell you, if I'd had a bottle of that old Bacchanalia in front of me I'd of taken a good, big slug of it right then. I guess I'd rather be sick as a dog than have a girlfriend.

10

The next morning the word I randomed when I woke and got dressed was "scabrous." A pitiful way to start the day! A "scabrous" is an "adj." so I looked up what an "adj." is, and its job is to describe a noun. So you might say: "The scabrous adj. said it was the ugliest noun he'd ever seen."

It is also something that is covered with warts and bumps and sores, so I guess if you have a name-calling adj. with warts and bumps and sores, you can call it a scabrous.

Anyway we'd no more than sat down to breakfast when a truck pulled up with the men to install the new indoor plumbing. A fellow with a sort-of white shirt knocked at the door, and Aunt Izzy brought him in and showed him where she wanted the indoor plumbing. His name wasn't actually "Actually," but that's the way I remember him because he couldn't say anything at all without saying it. They stood there, each of them waving their arms and pointing, like they might be arguing about the way to Tulsa. I went outside to get out of their way.

There were two more men out back of the house, and they'd stretched four long, tight strings between stakes. Each of them had a shovel and looked to be digging ditches right along those lines. Now, not wanting to brag, but I just do figure I know the difference between indoor plumbing and outdoor plumbing. And that, as the fellow says, looked to me like the outdoor variety was about to transpire.

"What are the ditches for?" I asked the red-faced digger. He looked friendly, and he was.

"Why, these are the laterals," he said, maybe with a touch of pride.

"Does my Aunt Izzy know you guys are digging up her back yard?"

I guess I maybe sounded a little feisty, because the red-faced fellow said, "Don't worry, Son. We'll fill them with gravel and cover them with dirt and nobody will know the difference."

Well, by grab! If that wasn't the dumbest thing I'd ever heard! You didn't have to be old Sherlock Holmes to know that these guys were plain and simple grifters. They were charging Aunt Izzy to dig ditches in her own backyard so they could fill them with gravel and then hide the evidence.

I wanted to whip them both right then and there, but I knew I couldn't. They were both big and strong and armed with shovels. I was smart enough to know that the most dangerous thing in the world is an Italian or an Irishman armed with a shovel. So I just went on my way, whistling a merry tune like they would expect a dumb kid to do. A kid who figured it was perfectly natural to have people coming—six days a week and twice on Sunday—to bury gravel in the backyard. My butt!

Aunt Izzy would be cleaning *their* plows mighty soon.

I found another fellow crawling around in the dirt under the house. He had a lantern and I could see he was trying to hook up some water pipes. Still and all, he was mostly just cussing, and for a quick moment I wished old Pauline was a boy so I could wish she were there. I'd like for her to witness a fellow getting paid for what she enjoyed doing for free.

About then Aunt Izzy called me. She was leaving the indoor plumbing people to do their work and figured we might as well do a little work in the garden before it got too hot. We put on our straw hats. She got a hoe and I found my potato bug coal oil can. Those old bugs had been there sitting in the sun for a good long time, and they looked to be about as dead as potato bugs are likely to get.

Now I'm not a person who gets all teary-eyed over everything that's dead. Not like girls do. Not over every dang dead bird and cat and butterfly. But there's something about a pile of dead potato bugs that seems sort of sad to me. What I'm telling you is, I know a little about being Presbyterian. And if you're Presbyterian your life is what they call predestinated. So if you're a potato bug and God has decided you'll end up in a can of coal oil, then you just as well not worry too much about if you'll make the football team.

Nevertheless, I figured a quick prayer on their behalf wouldn't hurt—if nobody saw me, so I did. "Oh Lord, please bless these dead potato bugs to the strength of our soul and body. In the name of Him who taught us to say when we pray, 'Ahem.'"

Truth to tell, I did feel a little peculiar, just turning right around and drowning a bunch more of those little bugs in coal oil, but there wasn't a thing

I could do about it. It wasn't my fault they were Presbyterian.

So I worked along, row after row, and I wondered if Jesus ever picked potato bugs. If He did, did He drop them in a can of coal oil like His Dad predestined them, or did He just miracle them to death and go sit in the shade of a piss elm tree?

By and by Aunt Izzy declared she'd had enough of the heat and we went inside. She chipped ice for the tea and poured herself a little "sidecar" of giggle water.

"Is that giggle water or Bacchanalia?" I asked. I sure didn't want Aunt Izzy to get a bad headache like I'd had.

"Why, Jefferson," she admonished. (She used my whole name, which is Jefferson, so's I'd know she was serious.) "It's way too early in the day to drink Bacchanalia!"

About that time the indoor plumbing boss came in and invited us to come have a look. He said the job wasn't actually finished, because nothing had actually been hooked up yet, but we could see how it was going to look.

Well, how it looked was *grand!* They had laid new linoleum, and the big old bathtub was about the size of a Pierce Arrow and just as shiny. There was a tag on it that said "Guaranteed perfect in every way." I don't guess you could wear that tub out in a million years of Saturdays. It had feet that were claws, and they seemed to be holding tight to that new linoleum. A dang giant couldn't move it if it didn't want to be moved!

The sink turned out to actually be a "lavatory," and the post it sat on was actually a "pedestal." I had no idea I'd have to learn so much to use indoor plumbing!

But the plumber saved the best until last: the toilet. I kinda didn't want to even look at it, what with Aunt Izzy being there and all, but he seemed so proud of it, I didn't want to hurt his feelings. The truth of it is, I wasn't sure I would ever be able to use that beautiful thing as a privy. He pointed out that the lid and the water tank, which was clear up under the ceiling, were actually pure "quarter sawn oak," and the tank was lined with actually solid copper so it wouldn't leak in a million years.

There was a chain with a wooden hand-grip hanging down from the tank, and the fellow explained that "when the time comes, you just pull that chain and it 'flushes.'" I sort of got the picture, but I wasn't really sure I'd *know* when the time came.

Now, the older I get, the more difference I see in adults and kids. Not that I'm much of a kid anymore. I'll be twelve before long; on the 19th of August, in fact. I was born, as Grandma sometimes says, "In the year of our Lord" 1926. I don't know why they call it the Lord's year. He wasn't born in 1926. I was the one born in 1926, so they ought to call it The Year of Jefferson Davis Johnson. But nobody ever does.

Anyway, like I started to say, adults can just talk the antlers off any subject you name. And flushing toilets is not the least of these, my brethren. To hear Aunt Izzy and the indoor plumbing man, there are details and subtleties and glories beyond belief to be found with the pull of a chain.

When the grocery delivery kid banged on the back door I could have kissed him. I was saved, rescued. I could only hope I wouldn't be around when they actually got *water* in the dang thing. I excused myself, hoping they hadn't noticed my red face, and got out of there.

I guess if I had that delivery job I would be the

happiest fellow in the world. All he does all day is drive the "Ted's IGA" Model A Ford truck around town delivering people's groceries. And he gets paid for it! I'd be *returning thanks* to get to do it for free. I'd drive right up to the Potts' house and blow the horn and old Pauline would come running out and slap her forehead and say: "sumbich."

The IGA guy brought in a box of groceries, set them on the kitchen counter and let the door slam shut on his way out. I started unpacking. The second thing I pulled out was a package of Animal Crackers. Aunt Izzy had bought them for me! Animal Crackers! She still thought I was a kid!

"Judas Priest!" It felt so good, I said it again, *"Judas Prr-iest!"*

The day before Aunt Izzy had hung the ice sign on the front porch, and I'd got introduced to Tony the iceman. He was kind of hunched from carrying all that heavy ice and looked to be about as old as Aunt Izzy.

Still and all, Aunt Izzy had gotten a lot younger since I'd been here. Younger than when I saw her with her nose intimate with the screen door. "Intimate" is when you push your nose against a screen door and get rust on it. Your nose.

Tony was kind of dark skinned and had a mustache like a Hungarian. But I only know one Hungarian. He lives back home in Epic and also has a wooden leg, just like Mose Washington, so I guessed Tony may not be a Hungarian.

Anyway, Aunt Izzy greeted him with a "Hey, Daddy-o! How's it hangin'?"

Tony gave her a big grin and said, "Fair and square, Kiddo."

Aunt Izzy held the icebox lid open and Tony set

the big block of ice in, then sleeved the sweat from his forehead.

"It's hot as a Turkish bath out there," he said.

Okay, I thought, if he knows how hot a Turkish bath is, he must be a Turk. I wondered if Turks take their baths in a wash tub under a peach tree like I do. Sometimes that's pretty hot.

Aunt Izzy chipped some ice from the new block and said, "You just need a little drinky poo-avous to cool yourself off."

"That'd be just the ticket-avous," he agreed.

I'll tell you, by that time I'd about reached the conclusion that my presence was not really required. Suddenly, I developed a great desire to do some whistling—outside.

I eased quietly toward the door, but I needn't have bothered being quiet. And if anybody noticed me going, they didn't bother to wish me a von boyage.

After supper we sat in the parlor, me and Aunt Izzy. She hadn't had a chance to read the *Buffalo County Trans-Weekly Disciplinarian*, what with all the digging and banging. We both sat with our feet propped up, sipping our cold drinks. I wasn't really asleep—just resting my eyes, as the fellow says—when Aunt Izzy let out a whoop that scared the bejesus out of me and made me wish the indoor plumbing was finished.

"He did it!" she squealed. "Good old Joe Lewis beat Max Schmeling in two minutes and four seconds! This calls for a little drinky poo!"

Now, it's just a guess on my part, but I'd bet if Schmeling had knocked out Joe Lewis, a drinky poo would have still been in order, if only to honor our Fallen Hero.

We were both bone tired from the excitement of

the day. Aunt Izzy suggested we go to bed a little early, and I didn't argue. Indoor plumbing can just wear a fellow out.

I dragged myself upstairs to my bedroom, undressed and turned out the light. I lay there and, without a reason in the world, started wondering if the indoor plumbing people had gotten their ill-gotten gravel covered up. It didn't matter, not a bit. Still and all, you can't go to sleep not knowing.

I looked out the open window and the gravel was all covered like they promised. But it wasn't the ungravel that grabbed my eye. There, moving across the moonlit backyard with an unlit lantern, was Aunt Izzy. And trailing right behind her came a long line of what looked for all the world like a warpath of Indigenous Rudolph cats.

There's a difference between walking and sneaking, and Aunt Izzy wasn't sneaking. When you're sneaking you sort of try to look invisible, even though you know you're not. You keep looking over your shoulder like there might be a bear or an alligator back there—or more likely, the Hardy Boys, out spying again. And if the sneaker is a man in a derby hat, it's likely a ghost. Aunt Izzy wasn't wearing a derby, so I knew she hadn't ghosted on me. She wasn't really hurrying, but she wasn't stopping to look for four-leaf clovers, either.

It wasn't like the Aunt Izzy I knew, or thought I knew, to go out walking amongst the rattlesnakes and devil claws in the dark of night. And carrying an unlit lantern wasn't exactly "the bee's knees." Still and all, I knew I couldn't holler and ask what in the world she was doing. It was her business, her home. Maybe that's just what Matriarchs do, but she was headed for the mine. A shiver raced my back.

I watched her out of sight, and then I watched

where she had been. If she lit the lantern, I couldn't see it.

I hadn't noticed much breeze before, but I had me a case of the goose bumps then. It crossed my mind to wonder if the Hardy Boys ever stood around in their underpants watching a mysterious moon-light-walker until they got goose bumps. If they did, I expect their mom had warned them to be sure and wear clean ones in case they were nabbed by a mysterious moonlight-walker.

Well, the dang Hardy Boys could stand there and freeze in their underpants if they wanted to. I went back to bed; it was a long time before I went to sleep.

11

I'd already randomed my word for the day when I remembered Aunt Izzy's rambling. The word was "cuke." Cucumber! If there was a dumber word to put in a dictionary I couldn't imagine what it might be. Still and all, it would be easier to work into a conversation than "ostrich."

For instance, a fellow might say, "I danged near stepped on a cucumber" and get by with it. Try that with an ostrich!

A "wafting" is something that happens in the air that you can't see, sort of like an amoeba. Except you can smell one, which you can't an amoeba. Anyway, one was happening as I was pulling on my pants and shirt, and it almost had to be a breakfast one. Yet it wasn't a bacon and eggs waft, or a pancake one, either. In fact, it smelled exactly like a cookie waft.

Aunt Izzy was already sitting at the table, and she had poured a hot cup of coffee for each of us.

Now see, that's another thing I loved about Aunt

Izzy. She just took it as a natural fact of life that I drank coffee. There wasn't any of this "you're too young" or "it will stunt your growth" stuff. That was just like Aunt Izzy.

What wasn't like Aunt Izzy was, she wasn't... maybe, quite like Aunt Izzy. What I'm trying to say is, she wasn't like the *Matriarch* Aunt Izzy, and she wasn't like the jazz-talking, dancing Aunt Izzy, either. She was there, but she was also, kind of, somewhere else.

"I thought we might have a little change for our breakfast today," she said. She whisked a napkin off a big plate of cookies and said, "Te Dum!" I knew I should act surprised, so I did. But, shoot, I can smell cookie-waft a mile away.

By the time I'd started on my fourth one, Aunt Izzy was smiling big.

"Jesse's taken a liking to you, Jeffie. He figured you might like some of his famous 'Train Robber' cookies." So he picked out a whole pail of hickory nuts and, last night, he baked them up."

Well, of course I hadn't mentioned a word about seeing her going out last night, or about her looking all smudgy and tired this morning. Still and all, she had cleared up some of the mystery—but only some of it.

"Did you really say that Jesse James *likes* me? He don't even know me. He's been sort of...well... sort of dead for a thousand years."

For the tiniest second a sly look passed over Aunt Izzy's face. Then she squeezed her eyes shut and gave her head a hard shake, like she was bringing her mind back from someplace else.

"Oh, Jeffie, sometimes my mouth just seems to run away. What I mean is, I know Jesse *would* like you if he had a chance. And he'd want to bake you some of his cookies too. See, to make them right, you have to bake them in his old oven, right there in the mine. I think there's something about the air in that place that makes them so special. I asked my neighbor, Eugene, to chop some kindling to start the fire, so it wasn't any trouble."

I knew the neighbor she was talking about was old Indigenous Dennis's brother, Aborigine Eugene. The same Aborigine Eugene she'd told me wouldn't go near the mine.

Maybe she was reading my mind, because the next thing she said was, "Eugene doesn't like that place at all. He says there's spirits there. So he only brings the kindling up to about thirty feet from the entrance, and I have to take it on in."

Thank goodness my good Presbyterian manners took over just then—took over from the bad thoughts that Aunt Izzy had gone a little dingy on me.

"Why, I'd be happy to carry that kindling in for you any old time," I told her. "These are the best cookies I ever had in my life!"

Aunt Izzy gave me the big smile she always uses, and said, "Jesse is right about you. You are a good-hearted boy."

Now look, I hadn't lived in this old world for almost twelve years without learning the difference between "is" and "was." And it was plain to see that, to Aunt Izzy's way of thinking, Jesse James was an "is," not a "was."

"I declare, Jeffie, I feel worn out already this morning; I think I'm getting old."

"Go ahead and take a nap," I told her, "I'll wash the dishes, and then I think I'll check on the cukes."

"The what?"

"The cukes," I told her. "It's a dictionary word for cucumbers."

She smiled, but not much, and raised her eyebrows at the same time. It's not as easy as it sounds. When she left the room I tried it. It works best if you raise your eyebrows before you try to add the smile.

I was feeling pretty good about my new accomplishment when there was a peck-pecking on the window of the kitchen door. I'll likely never know which of us got the worst surprise: him, the guy standing outside, naked from the waist up, looking ugly as a run-over turtle, or me, caught unaware, trying to smile with my eyebrows raised.

He knocked again, harder this time, with his knuckle. I opened the door wondering if it might be the last door I ever opened. When I saw his tomahawk, I knew I was a gonner. Sumbich! This had to be Aborigine Eugene!

I knew exactly how old Casey Jones felt just before the train wreck...with something warm running down his overalls.

Now what I found out was this—and I know it likely wouldn't work the same for everybody—but my life did not flash before my eyes. I didn't see any long, dark tunnel with a bright light at the end. I didn't see a band of Heavenly Hosts or a host of Heavenly Bands or whatever it is you're supposed to see. In that last few seconds of my life I saw the front page of *The Buffalo County Trans-Weekly Disciplinarian:*

"Brave lad dies in futile attempt to save sort of dingy Great Aunt! Aborigine Eugene commits savage amokery!"

Without a thought in my head I grabbed that plate of cookies and shoved them in his hand. "Ah...ah... Aunt Izzy told me to be sure and give you these," I stuttered.

Now you may be thinking what I did was an act

of Presbyterian charity. *Bull hockey!* I was trying to save my Presbyterian scalp!

He took the plate of cookies and never cracked a smile. He just said, "Thank you." I knew he had mastered the art of civilized restraint but really wanted to say "Ugh, Paleface."

"Tell Miss Isabella I finished chopping the kindling."

Well, right there before my eyes that old blood lust seemed to melt away. I explained that Aunt Izzy was taking a nap, but I would be sure to tell her about the kindling. He gobbled a cookie by way of reply, then stood there, looking for all the world like a cigar store wooden Aborigine.

You've doubtless heard that old saying "music soothes the savage breast." Well, I'm here to tell you, when it comes to good old-fashioned savage-breast-soothing, music is small potatoes compared to Train Robber cookies. With that first cookie I believe all thoughts of blood curdlery drained out of old Aborigine Eugene, and I deemed it likely behooved me to admit to a little hospitality.

I already told you about behoovery, but if you don't know a "deem," it works about the same as an "I figure." On the other hand, if you add an "ed" it's a past participle so there's not much need worrying about it. It's already too late.

Looking back, I probably should have invited him into the parlor. That's where Aunt Izzy takes company, but I was smart enough to remember that beaded curtain hanging in the doorway. There's nothing in the world that stirs up a wild Indian like beads. And I didn't figure (see, here I could have said, "deemed," but I'd about had it with past participles) there was enough difference between an Indian and an Aborigine to take the chance. So I

pointed to a chair at the kitchen table and said, "Si-
tum."

And he did. I was tickled to death to find I could
speak a little Aborigine, and also that he was smart
enough to understand it.

"Aborigine brother likeum little drinky poo-
avous?" I asked. But before he could answer, I was
already setting the jar of Bacchanalia and a clean
glass in front of him. I knew Aunt Izzy would approve, but I sort of deemed he'd prefer a gourd or a
buffalo horn to a glass. Still and all, I wasn't about
to turn my back on him to go digging through the
cupboard to find where Aunt Izzy kept her gourds
and buffalo horns.

I will certainly have to admit that old Aborigine
Eugene knew a thing or two about his manners. He
filled that glass like he'd used one all his life, and
never said a grumbling word.

I expect a fellow could teach an Aborigine some
good tricks if you got one when he was young and
you had the patience.

He lifted that glass of Bacchanalia to his lips and
paused, "I do hope you will join me," he said.

Just like that! "I do hope you will join me!" I don't
suppose the king of New Mexico could have said it
any nicer.

I'm smart enough to know it's an insult to
refuse to have a drink when a fellow asks you,
and it's even worse if he happens to be an Aborigine. Why, it couldn't be any worse if you spit in an
Aborigine's potato salad.

Now, I'm not going to brag and let on as if I've
see a lot of picture shows because I haven't. My
dad says they cost money, therefore they're against
God's will. Seems like, to my dad, just about
anything that costs money is against God's will

unless it's something *he* wants to do. I mean my
dad, not God. I expect God can go to the picture
show free and per gratis. And get free popcorn too.

Anyway, what I'm trying to say is, it would have
been more right if Aunt Izzy had a bar and a brass
rail to rest my boot on, even though I was barefoot
at the time.

And the bad cowboy would say, "I don't drink
with no stinkin' Aborigine." But if the picture show
is a "serial," you'll have to come back every Saturday
even if you have to steal the money for a ticket, because there's no dang way but what that cowboy is
going to suffer death and disfigurement at the hands
of the disgruntled and insulted Aborigine.

So it was, likely, just as well Aunt Izzy didn't
have a bar or a brass rail.

I told Mr. Aborigine Eugene I would be proud to
have a drink with him, and told him I usually preferred a little Kool-Aid with my Bacchanalia. He looked
at me a little funny, but I got the pitcher of Kool-Aid
from the icebox and poured some in my glass. "Red
brother likum Kool-Aid in Bacchanalia-um?"

He looked at me a little askance, and nodded his
head.

An "askance" is how you look when something is
beyond belief. I'm not really sure if Aborigines even
believe in Kool-Aid, but I was pleased he was game
to try.

I'll say this about old Eugene: he wasn't much of
a talker, but he could hold his liquor! So I set about
to make him comfortable and take his mind off his
savage heritage.

"I sure enjoy reading about your ancestors," I told
him. "Good old Aborigine Alley Oop and his squaw,
Ooola. They're the cat's pajamas."

To tell the truth, he didn't seem to have much

interest in ancestors *or* pajamas—even about Ooo-la, whom I considered to be a cat's pajama on her own recognizance. Then I suggested we sign a peace treaty and bury the hatchet, and that didn't seem to be on his agenda, either; but I think I saw his eyes blink.

I suppose it must be pretty hard for a simple Aborigine to keep his mind on more than one thing at once, and Eugene's mind was more or less obligated on his glass and the plate of Train Robber cookies.

It wouldn't be quite fair to lead you to think I was not doing my share in cookie eating and Bacchanalia/Kool-Aid drinking. I was plain not about to let an Aborigine think he could outdo a native born American boy.

As it turned out, old Aborigine Eugene was a pretty good fellow. If old Columbus had just filled the Aborigines up with Kool-Aid and Bacchanalia at the beginning, I deem it would have saved a lot of pilgrims and other palefaces from a bloody demise.

Well, good old Aborigine Eugene was getting nicer by the minute, and I'd just as well tell you, I was getting pretty nifty myself. I knew my dad wouldn't approve of the company I was keeping; he preferred friends with a white predilection.

Anyway, next thing I asked him was, "Have you killed a heap of buffalo?"

He shook his head, and I believe there was a little sadness there. He said, "No, but I nearly choked on a buffalo nickel when I was five."

Now, it's only fair to give a fellow a chance to redeem his failure, so I said, "Seen any ostriches lately?"

He scratched his head and finally admitted, "No, but I once watched a fellow cut his toe off with an ax."

I'll admit to a little disappointment. Still and all, my mind was getting agiler and agiler.

"Now, I mean no offense, Mr. Eugene, but do your people still hold a grudge against Custer?"

That one just about got him flummoxed.

"Why, I never heard of it if they do. I can't imagine why anyone would hold a grudge against custard, it's mostly just eggs. Fact is, I enjoy a good cup of custard now and again.

Now, I honestly believe old Eugene was trying his best to show his race in a good light, but enough is enough. I wouldn't embarrass my new buddy any further.

Luckily, about that time Aunt Izzy came through the door and the nap had done her a world of good. She fair sparkled when she saw old Aborigine Eugene and me sitting there together.

Old Aborigine Eugene tried to stand and greet her, but his Aboriginal nimbleness had become a paucity, and his mannerly intent was a plethora of failure nearing on disaster.

"Oh, keep your seat," she told him. And she pushed him back into near upright. "Well, Jefferson, I'm proud to see you have offered Eugene our hospitality."

"Yes, ma'am," I told her. I took her advice myself and didn't try to stand. She took a chair there with us at the table and pulled the cookie plate closer. There were only three left, but the Bacchanalia jar was about half full. And there was a surprising lot of Kool-Aid in the pitcher.

Aunt Izzy didn't usually mix her drinks, but in the spirit of good fellowship and continuity, she added just a tinge of Kool-Aid to hers. She raised her glass and said, "Here's to the great state of Kansas, the home of indoor plumbing."

We all took a drink and Eugene lifted his glass, "Here's to custard."

Aunt Izzy gave him a look, but took another drink.

Then it was my turn. I raised my glass and said, "Here's to cukes." Old Eugene was flat nonplused but, being the good fellow he was, he would have drank to an alfalfa sandwich.

Aunt Izzy did her best to catch up with Eugene and me, and by grab if she wasn't doing a spectacular job of it. I was only taking small sips because I was getting a plan. She raised her glass and offered a salute to The Confederate States of America. We all joined in.

Aborigine Eugene's turn came again as was only right and proper. "To custard!" he said.

"But we've already drank to custard," Aunt Izzy protested.

"Well, I shay cushtard and I mean cushtard!" His voice was a little louder and, inadvertently or not, his hand inched toward his tomahawk.

"Here's to cushtard," I cried.

Aunt Izzy was a good sport and admitted this drink was for cushtard.

She'd sort of forgot it was my turn next and said, "Here's to Jesse James, the only man I ever loved... loved and lost." Tears started down her cheeks.

Aborigine Eugene raised his glass and said, "Absholutly! And here's also to the only girl I ever loved an' lost. I don't remember her name."

"My soul and body, Eugene, I didn't know you had lost your one true love. Was she shot like my Jesse?"

Eugene waved that thought away. "No, no, not shot. Not that kind of lost. Jusht mishplaced. I put her in Enid, Oklahoma, and now I can't find her."

So with tears rolling, they drank to their lost loves and then called down the wrath of God on St. Joseph, Missouri, and Enid, Oklahoma.

While they fell into discussing what should be toasted next, I slyly stood up and absconded the tomahawk behind my back. I asked to please be excused, but nobody noticed. I sort of fumbled my way out the door and down the steps, and got almost to the spirea bush before I puked my guts out.

I made my way to the garden, lifting each foot high because...well, because you never know. The garden was pretty much where it was supposed to be, and I scooped out a little hole amongst the cucumbers. I buried that old tomahawk, patted the dirt over it, and felt safe for the first time all day.

Now, not to put my native brothers down in any way shape or form, but I knew old Aborigine Eugene would never find it. An Aborigine wouldn't know a "cuke" if it bit him on the ankle.

12

I woke next morning. Sort of. Still sleepy, but feeling better than I had any right to, what with all that Bacchanalia and all. Maybe I was getting to be, as the fellow says, "a man who can handle his liquor." I knew my dad would be proud of the way Aunt Izzy was leading me toward the embracement of manhood.

I also knew that my best friend, old Purdy Grundy, would be eating his heart out when I told him about my adventures of yesterday. Starting with a breakfast of Train Robber cookies, followed by foiling a bloodthirsty Aborigine insurrection single-handedly by my bravery and by my unselfish willingness to sacrifice any hope of redemption by imbibing the demon rum for the good of all.

Of course I'd never mention to Purdy how old Daniel Boone would have given his right arm to have a fellow like me along in his adventures. I'm not one to brag, and anyway it'd work better if Purdy believed he thought of it himself.

So I lay there thinking—how it might have been:

I woke on the cold ground. Ol' Dan'l was asleeping right aside me, and snoring like a dang buzz-saw. "Dan'l, for pity sakes, your noise will have them Aborigines down on us in no time at all!"

Well, then old Dan'l would sort of roll over and say, "Why thank you, young Jefferson Davis Johnson. You have likely saved my scalp."

And then he'd say, "By grab, I'd give up my hope for redemption for a good chew. Don't reckon you've got a extra, do you?"

I would lay aside my trusty rifle, which was longer than I was all stretched out, and say, "Just happen I do, Dan'l. My mom packed up fourteen pounds of 'baccky ere we started this here adventure. First, she was a little afraid to because of the immense cost, but my dad says, 'Hang the expense, this is the Lord's work!'"

And about that time a fierce redskin would stick his head up from the treacherous larkspur vines and say, "Ugh, Paleface."

And I'd say, "Ugh right back to you, you varmint!"

And old Dan'l would pat me on the shoulder and say, "I guess you told him, young Jefferson Davis Johnson."

And then I'd invite them all in for a little drinky poo-avous and give each one a jar of Bacchanalia. The chief would shake my hand and say, "Holy cow! That's more than we got for Manhattan Island and the five Boroughs!"

Meantime, while they were all getting happy and bemoaning the loss of the only girls they ever loved, I would steal their tomahawks.

And then I'd say, with a great deal of emotion in my voice, "Quick, Dan'l, where is the nearest cuke patch?"

And he would say, "You don't need no patch. If you're gonna puke, just go ahead and puke!"

And then I'd say, "Dagnab it, Dan'l, you got beans in your ears? I said cuke, c-u-k-e!"

And old Daniel Boone would say, "Just what under the light of the living sun are you a-talking about? What is a cuke?"

And I would think—but never say aloud— "Dan'l, you ain't a great deal smarter than a dang Aborigine!"

So, after I took the valuable time to explain what the heck a cuke was, ol' Dan'l would say, "Well, hell, young Jefferson Davis Johnson, why didn't you just say 'cucumber'? There is a whole passel of them right over there yonder!"

So I would bury the tomahawks under the cucumbers as per the rules "according to Hoyle."

Then all the settlers would rush up an' shake my hand and say, "Young Jefferson Davis Johnson, you have saved us again. And we shall build an obelisk seven feet high of the finest stone, in your honor."

And then a sort of cute girl with black hair named Pauline, would run up and give me a kiss on the cheek and whisper in my ear, "sumbich."

...Aunt Izzy called again, "Jeffie? Are you dead up there? I've called you fifteen times! Breakfast's ready."

Not even taking time to random my word for the

day, I pulled on my shirt and britches and went down to the kitchen.

As always, Aunt Izzy set a bowl of hot, boiled Grape Nuts in front of me and poured me a cup of coffee. I suppose it was a comfort to know I wasn't going to get the diphtheria from eating raw Grape Nuts, but the truth is—I don't remember that part.

Something had been itching at my mind since the day before, and I knew I shouldn't ask but I plain couldn't help myself.

"Aunt Izzy, would you get mad if I ask you a question?"

"Well, of course not," she said, "You can ask me anything you want."

"Well, please don't take it wrong, and I probably misunderstood, but was...I mean *is*...Jesse James your boyfriend?"

Aunt Izzy stepped to the cupboard, brought out the jar of giggle water and mixed some with her breakfast coffee. She sort of looked at her bowl of boiled Grape Nuts, and sighed. "I was afraid it would come to this, but it's all right. The answer is yes, Jeffie. I suppose you could say he's my boyfriend...has been all my life. I've had lots of boys as friends, but Jesse is always special."

I'll tell you, that was a jolt. So I asked her, did that mean Jesse James could have been my great uncle?

She shook her short, Louise Brooks hair and laughed. "Jesse has a strong, masculine voice," she said, "but not *that* strong!

"First time I met Jesse was when he saved my life. I was fourteen, and taking some cold lemonade to my brother, Willard, up at the mine. Like a silly kid I wasn't paying any attention where I was going and, all of a sudden, a loud voice cried, 'Isabella, STOP!' Scared me to death. But when I looked at where I was about to step, I was scared a lot worse. There was a big old rattlesnake lying right in the path, and I would have stepped on him sure if Jesse hadn't called my name. Makes me shiver to think of it."

"Holy cow, Aunt Izzy, how did Jesse James know your name?"

"I never knew, Jeffie. Sometimes we just have to believe."

"That's for sure. Did I tell you my whole family is Presbyterian?"

"I believe you mentioned that, yes. Anyway, Jesse knew, and ever since we've been buddies and visit all the time."

"Speaking of snakes," I offered, "that old Pauline told me she's got a snake. She says it's nine feet long and as big around as her arm, except she's probably lying. She says she looked it up in a snake book, and it's called "A Highly Poisonous Kansas Double-Breasted Egg-Sucker." It's a big, black snake that lives in the barn and eats rats and eggs. But she's probably lying. She says it's real tame; she can set an egg just a few inches from his nose, then sit real still, and that old snake will come right up an' gobble that egg right in front of her."

"Yeah, she's probably lying," Aunt Izzy agreed. "Dang girls. Pity she's not a boy so you could believe her."

"I know. I wisht she were, because she invited me over to see it, but I'll bet she doesn't have a snake because her arms aren't very big around anyway."

"Well, Jeffie, it's a shame, but that's the way girls are. Yuck. 'Course, I guess if a fellow wasn't afraid of big snakes, and really wanted to see one eat an egg, he could just ignore Pauline. Just pretend she wasn't even there. And when he was through snake-watching, he could just go home."

We rid the table and washed the dishes. Meanwhile, I was thinking.

I told Aunt Izzy I hadn't yet randomed my word for the day, and she told me to run along and do it.

So I dug out my dictionary and randomed my new word. It was a blessing that Virgil, my dog, hadn't peed on it. The word was "propitious," which looks like it should be said with a "pity" but it should be said with a "pish." That is because the English language is made up by a bunch of Frenchmen, Latiners, Greeks and more others than you would think possible. Probably Methodists too. My dad says if you want a thing screwed up royally, give it to a Methodist.

Anyway, "propitious" means "auspicious," which turns out to be not as bad as you might think, because "auspicious" just means "favorable" so why the heck don't they just say, "favorable?"

Still and all, "propitious" would be a handy word to use, even though it is a stupid word. And see, if a fellow had some time on his hands and wanted an "antonym"—which, like I told you, is the word that is just opposite—it would be "bad." And the word, "sumbich" is bad, so if you had to, you could say, "Unpropitiously, the ostrich awoke to find himself motley, and that was a pure sumbich."

Downstairs I found Aunt Izzy as giddy as a dang girl. "Shall I call Mrs. Potts and ask if it's all right for you to come play with Pauline and see the snake?"

"No, ma'am," I told her, "It'd be more propitious if you ask her can I come *see* Pauline and play with the *snake*."

So without anymore adieu, Aunt Izzy rang Central and told her to please ring Mrs. Potts because Jefferson Davis wanted to see if she really had a snake in her barn. They talked for about two-and-a-half hours about how just awful it would be to have a snake in your barn.

Central talked really loud because you never know when you might have a "long distance," and I could hear every word. She told Aunt Izzy about one time there was a rattlesnake on her back porch and she hollered at her husband, Lester, and said, "Lester, come quick! There's a rattlesnake on the back porch!" And Lester came and said he weren't going anywhere near that damn snake, so she opened the screen door and threw the new aluminum pressure-cooker at it and scared it away. So she guessed it was worth it.

Anyway, Central finally gave up talking and rang Mrs. Potts. I expect *they* talked another two-and-a-half hours before they reached an auspicious decision and Aunt Izzy hung up the phone.

So finally, I told Aunt Izzy I guessed I'd mosey on over, then. But Aunt Izzy said, "Jeffie, you put your shoes on first or you'll step on a nail and get lockjaw."

Well, it began to look like I'd be drawing my Old Age Pension before I got to see the stupid snake, but I put my shoes on and eventually hit the dusty trail.

Old Pauline was standing in the front yard, just like I expected, with her fists on her hips like people do when they're going to say: "Well! It's about time!"

And she did.

I took Aunt Izzy's advice and ignored her. "Where's the snake?" I purposed.

She said, "You still got funny ears."

"Well, was I supposed to call the indoor plumbing people and have them remodeled just for you?"

She nodded her head toward the barn and I went along beside her. When we were out of sight of the house she pulled out two cigarettes and gave me one.

"Did you steal these?" I asked.

"Not that it's any of your business," she said, "but I made them."

"In a pig's eye you did," I disclaimed.

"I did! My dad had a cigarette-making machine and now it's mine. You just put in a paper, lick it, add some tobacco, pull the lever thing and, poof, out comes a cigarette.

I told her I had to stop rolling my own cigars because we were getting indoor plumbing.

When we got to the barn Pauline put her finger to her lips, which is Indian sign language for *Shhh!* We snuck in and she pointed to a crack where the sunlight was shining in on the floor, and whispered, *"There he is!"*

She pointed. But there he wasn't, at least no more than the last wriggle of him. "See!" she cried, "There's his butt!"

Well sir, a snake's butt may be a thing of beauty and a joy forever to a girl, but to a fellow who's just put down an Aborigine insurrection and buried a tomahawk with the cucumbers, it's considerable less than a religious experience.

"Come on!" she shouted, and she shot out of the barn door as determined as Martin and Osa Johnson trying to baptize a pygmy. Old Pauline ran pretty good for a girl.

Still and all, it was a complete waste of time. There's nothing more gone than a snake when it wants to be.

Pauline had her fists on her hipbones again. "It's your fault! You went charging in there like a dang elephant!"

"My fault?!" I outraged.

"You got beans in your ears? YOUR FAULT! You pea-brained cabbage head!"

Pauline was a great one for adding vegetables to her conversations.

She sat on the ground with her feet sort of tucked under, like Indians always do. Except, I suppose, if they're too old or their knees bother them if they sit on the ground.

"Maybe I should give him a name and train him to come when I call him," she said.

"You can't train a snake," I told her. "They're too dumb."

"Well, maybe *you* can't, but I can. Every time he does what I say, I'll give him an egg and say, "Good snake!" Every time he doesn't, I'll slap him in the chops and say, 'Bad snake!'"

Pauline looked serious as a midnight graveyard, and I could see that old snake had a mighty bleak future.

So we sat there. Pauline dug out two more pretty much uncrumpled cigarettes. She smoked and looked snake-disgusted. I just enjoyed a good smoke and considered how Pauline would look if she grew up to be a French lady.

13

By the time I got home, the sky was looking mean as sin. I found Aunt Izzy hoeing in the garden, trying to grub out the weeds before the rain came. I poured a little coal oil in my old potato bug can and fell in beside her.

Well, sir, there were more dang bugs than I'd ever seen! I'll tell you this, when the meek inherit the earth, they'll likely find the potato bugs have already eaten all the leaves off it. And while I was plucking them off, I couldn't help wondering if potato bugs were one of the miseries God let Satan visit on poor old Job. I figured not. Potato bugs don't just visit. When they come, they stay! Anyway, I've never seen a single mention of potato bugs in the Bible.

Still and all, if you're writing a Bible I don't expect they want to pay you to write about potato bugs.

Aunt Izzy was all ears to hear about my visit with Pauline. I told her about how the snake had elapsed through a crack so we only saw his butt. Aunt Izzy giggled, but I was serious. What I didn't tell her was how we'd smoked Pauline's cigarettes. And I didn't tell her about Pauline deeming old Jesse James had hidden some ill gotten treasure in his coal mine hideout.

"From what I've heard about Jesse James, the only 'treasure' you'll likely find are some old rusty Calumet baking powder cans," I'd told Pauline.

Anyway, Aunt Izzy was a little touchy talking about Jesse, so I didn't mention it.

The rain began to splatter big drops on the dusty ground, looking like fat spiders with skinny legs. Aunt Izzy and I sprinted for the house. Aunt Izzy shouted, "God causes the rain to fall on the just and the unjust!" I figured God had saved the lives of about a thousand potato bugs, and I hoped He was happy.

The indoor plumbing people were banging around, adding the last touches to the new bathroom. I plopped down at the kitchen table and Aunt Izzy chipped off some ice to make us drinks. She scarce had poured her drinky poo-avous when the telephone rang out longs and shorts. She rushed to the parlor and pretty quick called out in a teasing voice, "Oh, Jeffieee, It's for youuu. I think it's a gir-rllll." I hate it when someone uses that voice! It always means trouble.

And it was. Trouble. It was old Pauline. It had never crossed my mind that she might call me. I should have told her if she ever called me, and anyone answered—"*hang up.*"

Anyway, she told me she had named her snake. She had named it "Grandpa Porterfield" after her grandpa who had been declared "All-Time Champion Egg Sucker" at the annual egg-sucking contest at the Buffalo County Fair.

Pauline said she had taken four eggs to the barn

and found old Grandpa Porterfield sleeping in the crack-in-the-wall sun as usual. She laid an egg out a little in front of him and then kept real quiet. Pretty soon he ambled up to that egg and ate it right down. Still real quiet, she told him, "Good snake, Grandpa Porterfield. Good snake." Then she put out another egg. So pretty soon he ate that egg too, and she told him, "Good snake, Grandpa Porterfield! Good snake." And every time she put another egg out, he ate it and she told him, "Good snake, Grandpa Porterfield! Good snake."

So when Pauline ran out of eggs and started to leave, that old snake just naturally started to follow along. Pauline told him, "Sit, Grandpa Porterfield! Sit." But, of course snakes don't have butts to sit on. So when she realized her mistake, she said, "Stay, Grandpa Porterfield. Stay." And he did.

When we hung up I told Aunt Izzy about the snake and she said, "Why, for pity sakes! I had no idea Mrs. Potts was Mr. Porterfield's daughter. I remember when *The Buffalo County Trans-Weekly Disciplinarian* ran a front page article about him. He was egg-sucking champion for years. Until a fellow, named...I don't remember, Earl somebody-or-other, from over around Parsons—where almost everyone is named Earl—came here and beat him.

"That fellow, Earl, sucked down an even dozen eggs to Mr. Porterfield's eleven, accepted his blue ribbon, puked—some said 'grandly'—and went back home. There was some talk of giving him another blue ribbon for extemporaneous puking, but nothing ever came of it."

The remembrance of Mr. Porterfield and the Buffalo County Fair seemed to cheer Aunt Izzy's mood. We went back to the kitchen and she finished her drinky poo-avous and poured herself another. "I don't expect you ever heard about it, but I won a blue ribbon at that Fair once myself.

"See, I had a new boyfriend, Albert Brecheiser, and he was a dancing fool! We decided to enter the 'Charleston' dance contest at the fair, and we practiced and practiced until we had about created a new art form.

"When the big day came, we had incorporated the classic *pas de deux* the traditional *do-si-do*, then added a few steps of the *chicken-walk* for the kids. For the finale, Albert would do his own invention. He called it 'The Three Mayonnaise Squat.' It looked kind of dirty to me, and I thought he should call it 'The Diarrhea Dump.'

"I wore a long-waisted, flat-chested, flapper-style dress, which exposed my knees—that was all the rage in 1926. Albert wore his glen plaid jacket with checkered plus fours and argyle stockings. We were dressed to kill!

"The crowd went wild! But then, just as Albert went into his Three Mayonnaise Squat, my ex-boyfriend, Edgar, who was pitcher for the Buffalo Buffaloes, hurled a potato right at Albert's gonads. In a spectacular display of grace and ability, and without missing a beat, Albert snagged that potato, threw it back, as hard as he could, and knocked out two of Edgar's teeth.

"Albert grabbed my hand and we bowed and bowed to what seemed to be unending applause. It was one of the happiest days of my life!

"'Course, we won, hands down. And we took away the first prize of three dollars and the blue ribbon. As we went down the steps, a fellow came up and offered Albert a pitching job with the Epic Earthquakes."

Aunt Izzy couldn't seem to stop laughing at her

remembrances. She got up and poured herself another little drinky poo-avous and set the jar on
the table between us. I assumed the benefit of her
acknowledgement and dribbled a little into my
Kool-Aid.

She lit a cigarette, cocked her head and looked
at me. "I guess you smoke a little sometimes, don't
you, Jeffie?"

"Well, I burned down the privy, didn't I?" I didn't
mean to sound smart aleck at all, and if I did, Aunt
Izzy didn't seem to notice.

"Butt me," I said. We sat there, enjoying our cool
drinks and just smoking away. I would have given
up all my hope for redemption if old Pinky Smail and
Purdy Grundy could have seen me then.

About that time we heard the indoor privy flush,
and the indoor plumbing man stuck his head in the
kitchen. "All finished, ma'am. Want to take a look?"

He led the way down the hall like a grand parade marshal. Aunt Izzy was right behind him
and, after slugging down the last of my poo-avous
Kool-Aid, I followed. I expect that fellow couldn't
have been prouder were he cutting the ribbon to
open the Golden Gate Bridge. He pulled the chain
and Niagara Falls itself couldn't have made more
noise.

And that's when I realized I could never use the
indoor plumbing. It would be like bragging! It would
be like saying, "Look here, world. I've done it!" Pulling that chain would be calling the attention of everybody within forty miles to the fact that Jefferson
Davis Johnson had peed in the new indoor plumbing. Not this boy!

Now, maybe that indoor fellow was a little disappointed by our lack of enthusiasm. Maybe he
thought we had blinked and missed the show. He

pulled the chain again, and almost bowed. Even Aunt Izzy started to blush.

She thanked him sincerely and wrote him a check from her "Jesse James Hideout and Coal Mining Company" account.

We went back to the kitchen. Neither of us said a word, and we didn't stand on formality. Aunt Izzy poured some for her, and I poured some for me. She took a cig and scooted the pack to me. We both knew something had changed; it wasn't just the two of us now, there was me, and her, and IT.

There was a sort of feeling...like something should happen...like...I don't know. We were waiting. I took the biggest swig of poo-avous I ever had and commenced the ceremonies: I lifted my hands.

"And an angel of the Lord appeared unto them and saith, 'Fear not, for behold, I bring you tidings of great joy! For unto you this day, at the Jesse James Hideout and Coal Mining Company, a couple of miles south of the city of Armageddon, a Commode is given. And its name shall be called *Indoor Plumbing*.' And lo, a star appeared, and..."

Aunt Izzy let out a squeal of delight and threw the last of her poo-avous right in my face.

We laughed like a couple of fools, and when one of us would try to stop, the other would snicker and we'd start all over again. When she was able to catch her breath, Aunt Izzy threw her arms around me and said, "Jefferson Davis Johnson, you are the awfullest boy I ever met! And I love you to pieces."

Well, see, it wasn't long before I began to feel a certain pressure. The kind of pressure it's better to feel when you're outside. Aunt Izzy pretended not to notice as I went out the door and down the path to the privy.

As soon as I stepped back into the house, Aunt

Izzy was ready. One good turn deserves another, as the fellow says—so if Aunt Izzy used the outdoor privy that day you will never hear it from me.

Now here's a funny thing, Aunt Izzy had worked her tail off making the new indoor commode room a showplace. She'd hung fancy curtains in the window, put washcloths and towels by the bathtub and the pedestal lavatory; she'd hung two pictures: one, of those dogs playing poker, and the other, where the dejected Indian sits on his pony looking like he'd really like to find a bush to go behind.

There was a mirror above the pedestal lavatory, and beside it a medicine cabinet for things like Gimp, Mercurochrome, Carters Little Liver Pills and such.

My mom would have taken one look at that shiny linoleum floor and said, "Why, it's clean enough to eat off of." Now, I'm not telling you my mom went around looking for floors to eat off; I doubt she ever did. Still and all, had she been of a mind to, I expect this one would suit her just fine. As for myself, the floor didn't suit me at all. Where's the cracks for a fellow to drop his butts through? And where's the crack to spit through if you're sitting there and need to spit? Some fellows *do* take a little chew of tobacco occasionally, you know. Seems like it'd be a lot of bother to stand up and spit in the commode hole, sit back down, and have to jump right up again to spit again. And, if you are a beginner at indoor plumbing, you're just plain going to forget sometimes and spit on the floor. And the room was so bright! The honest truth is, it just didn't have the homey feeling of a privy.

We sat there at the table, me and Aunt Izzy, not like two people celebrating the joy of having indoor plumbing—more like two people who had shared a bottle of glumness.

I hadn't even used the dang thing yet, and here I was missing the morning glories that climbed and twined in the trellis and sort of sweetened the atmosphere around the good old privy. Maybe I could get Aunt Izzy to plant some friendly hollyhocks in pots along the hallway on the way to the indoor plumbing, to remind me of the good old days. And amongst the hollyhocks should be a great big old Wolf spider, with his web—dewy and sparkly in the sun. I'm not sure even Aunt Izzy would want a Wolf spider, but Wolf spiders don't bite.

Now, I've never been much of one to talk to myself, but I'll admit to sometimes passing the time of day with a spider or a mud dauber in the privy.

I wonder if anyone ever talks to a bathtub?

And there was always a roof leak in a privy, right above where you were sitting. And a fat, cold drop of rain would hit you on the back of your neck and cheer your whole day. When it was freezing cold, the icy wind would blow on your butt, so you couldn't just sit there and think about things, but you always knew you would have all summer to do your thinking, so it didn't matter.

When I looked at Aunt Izzy, I could tell she was having the same kind of thoughts, like she was reading my mind. She said, "Maybe I could find some hollyhock wallpaper for the hall, and right up by the commode room door I could hang some morning glory wallpaper."

"Could we get a little patch of wallpaper with a Wolf spider on it?" I asked.

"Wouldn't be much good without a Wolf spider," she admitted. "And I won't be able to stop on the way...I mean the way back—and admire my strawberries."

Aunt Izzy sighed into her glass.

"I'm sure gonna' miss that good old drip on the back of my neck," I told her. "Could we bore a hole in the roof?"

She pondered. "I could call the indoor plumbing man. Maybe he can run a little pipe out from the water tank and fix it so it will drip when no one is expecting it.

"Do you know what I'm really going to miss, Jeffie? What was really nice, was to sit there at night when you could leave the door open, and watch for falling stars. And you could hear the crickets screeching, and the locusts making their awful racket, and the bullfrogs *chuggerumphing*." She stared at her empty glass and shook her head. "It's gone forever," she sighed.

We were both long passed blushing at every little thing. It was more like "Old Settlers Day" at the Pleasant Valley Church, where the Good Old Times and the Bad Old Times, are remembered as the Best of Times.

"Do you reckon Jesse James used our old privy, Aunt Izzy?"

"No, sir." She paused to pour us another drink and tap out a cig for each. "I've looked and looked, and never found a trace of Jesse's privy. It's blown away like the sands of time...

"I'll tell you this, Jeffie, I'll be happy to use the new bathtub, but damned if I'll ever use that commode thing."

"Me either," I promised.

14

My word for the new day was "essence." And I guess that may be the most important word I ever randomed. Essence is what something really is.

See, I'd be proud to be the "essence" of Presbyterian. Aunt Izzy is the "essence" of nice, and Grandpa Porterfield is the "essence" of an egg-sucking snake. If you don't have an essence I doubt they'll ever let you into Business College.

When I got downstairs I found Aunt Izzy taking advantage of the cool of the morning in the garden. I would never in the world mention it when He was around to hear, but maybe God should have taken more days of rest than just Sunday. Seems to me if He'd gotten a little more sleep, He would have seen the reasonableness of having people eat weeds and potato bugs and grub out the vegetables. Maybe drop those pesky potatoes in a can of coal oil. It's a lot easier to grow weeds and potato bugs than it is to grow vegetables. Life would be easier that way. Still and all, I expect if you've got Good Samaritans tripping all over each other wanting to pick your potato bugs for you it would be easy to overlook things like that.

Aunt Izzy was a great one for making work look like fun. She'd go down the rows singing and "shaking that thing" 'til you'd of thought she was going to tramp those plants right into the ground. But she never did. And, of course I followed along picking potato bugs and shaking my own thing.

That's the way Pauline found us, me shaking my butt like a fool and hollering "Gotcha!" every time I plucked a potato bug.

I could have died!

She was carrying a basket of eggs, and as she got closer I could see that big old black snake, Grandpa Porterfield, wriggling along beside her like a best chum. When they reached the garden, Pauline took an egg between her thumb and finger. "Beg, Grandpa Porterfield. Beg." That old snake coiled himself up, raised his head, and plucked that egg from between her fingers like he was the King of England. "Good snake, Grandpa Porterfield!" she told him.

That was enough for Aunt Izzy who was a confessed snake hater. It was *too* much for the Rudolph cats who stood frozen with their fear-fur puffed out trying to look more fearsome than they felt. One Rudolph, the one we later named "Stumpy," made a dash for the only safety in sight: Aunt Izzy.

Now see, under normal circumstances, running to Aunt Izzy for safety would be the smartest thing in the world for a cat to do—but not when she was holding her hoe at full cock, and not when Aborigine Eugene had quietly stepped up behind her to tap her shoulder and inquire as to his lost tomahawk. I expect there is a lesson to be learned from what happened next; most likely more than one.

It wasn't Aunt Izzy's fault at all. If you've got a big egg-sucking snake in front of you, a shoulder-tapping Aborigine right behind you and a berserk cat climbing up your body like you were an Elm tree, it's blamed hard to pursue a normal life.

By the time old Rudolph reached the top of Aunt Izzy's head, I expect he realized he should have taken his chances with the snake. With one hand Aunt Izzy flung off the cat and with the other she brought down the hoe, unfairly asundering its tail, which was likely the only part of the cat that hadn't put a scratch on her.

Aunt Izzy tumbled back on her haunch, because a haunch is what a woman tumbles back on when she has just cut the tail off a snake-scared cat and been snuck up on by a shoulder-tapping Aborigine who lost his hatchet.

Old Stumpy, with his ears laid flat back on his head, gave a blind, howling leap and used his head to try to poke an escape hole through Aborigine Eugene's stomach. And that provoked Aborigine Eugene to perform an "Ugh" in his native tongue.

In a streak of mercy, Aunt Izzy dropped her hoe, grabbed the remnant of cat-tail and pursued the cat, graciously calling "Come back, Rudolph, come back." It was then I observed that cats, unencumbered by tails, are likely the second fastest creatures on earth. They are far and beyond faster than an Aunt Izzy, and almost as fast as a Pauline who mutters, "sumbich, sumbich, sumbich," with every flying step.

Pauline swept past me like the Super Chief, knocking my glasses off and grabbing old Stumpy just as he collided with the kitchen door. She held him tightly and soothed him by whispering, "sumbich, sumbich," in his ear.

While Aborigine Eugene stomped my only glasses

into the ground, cursing all white men clear back to Columbus's grandma and grandpa, Aunt Izzy jerked out one of her shoestrings and tied the tail-piece onto the stump of its original owner.

Now you would think a cat who had got his tail back might show a little Christian gratitude, but not old Rudolph. He seemed to want nothing to do with a tail that had deserted him when the going got tough. When Aunt Izzy stepped back to admire her tail-attaching, that old cat let it be known that it was not about to spend the rest of its life giving a free ride to a danged deserter. No sir, that old Rudolph grabbed a mouthful of his own dearly departed tail and yanked it back off quicker than quick.

Aunt Izzy, seeing her kindness rudely rejected, turned on her heel and announced that we should all, "just go cook a radish."

I felt behooved to compliment Pauline on her fast running, so I said, "Pauline, you run just as good as a boy!" She glared at me and sucker-punched me right in the belly.

I deemed it best not to tell her that she hit like one too.

15

Now, when Pauline raced off on her mission of cat-tail mercy, she left old Grandpa Porterfield all alone and, to any reasonable person's thinking, he became the sole caretaker of one mostly full basket of eggs.

For the next three days, Grandpa Porterfield belched. I'm talking the unplanned, unauthorized, unbiased freehand belching not likely heard since that old whale ate Jonah. But my dad always says, "'Tis better to burp and bear the shame, than not to burp and bear the pain."

If anyone was offended they didn't mention it, because if a fellow eats a whole basket of ignored eggs you can't, righteously, hold it against him if he becomes uncouth.

Pauline took it upon herself to accept credit for training that old snake to belch, but all she really did was a dereliction of her mom's eggs while she chased after a hoe-stricken cat. In my mind Grandpa Porterfield was just experiencing some plain old

Presbyterian egg-sucking guilt, but the truth is, after that when Pauline said "Belch, Grandpa Porterfield. Belch."—he did.

Old Pauline got all puffed up thinking she was the greatest snake trainer in the world, and Grandpa Porterfield himself began showing signs of having a high opinion of himself. If you would say, "Good morning, Grandpa Porterfield," he would belch. That's a little funny the first few times, but after a while a fellow just started feeling transgressed on.

Anyway, if I had done that at home I would have been packed off to reform school.

After a few days I got to wondering why I wasn't seeing much of Pauline so I deemed I'd go see what she was doing. I found her in the dark of her barn with the crack of sunlight showing right on Grandpa Porterfield. He was coiled up on a three-legged milking stool looking like a sap-headed fool.

Pauline was wearing four-buckle overshoes, holding a broken chair in one hand and an old buggy whip in the other—trying to look like a circus lion tamer. Well, I didn't mention it, but the barn wasn't *that* dark.

She did her best to crack that whip, but the best she could get out of it was a sort of a *whoosh*. Still and all, the whoosh was enough to make Grandpa Porterfield flinch and swallow hard.

I will tell you, if you set out to watch a snake swallow you don't have to be in a hurry because a snake is almost all throat and neck; a snake swallowing takes awhile. It's like, when God created the snake he held down too long on the make-a-neck button, and before He even got to the shoulders He ran out of snake meat.

So Pauline held her finger up to her lips, warning me to be quiet. I sat down as still as an Indigenous.

She tossed the chair aside and picked up a rusty hoop from a nail keg and cried, "Jump, Grandpa Porterfield. Jump on through!"

Grandpa Porterfield gave old Pauline a look that said more than if snakes had vocal cords. It was a *nuance* look, no two ways about it. All snakes have to use nuance looks because, like I said, they don't have vocal cords. There is no way to describe a nuance, but you'd better know what it is before you go messing around with snakes.

Anyway, I expect Grandpa Porterfield was years older than Pauline and, most likely, years smarter, too—though I'd never say that where Pauline could hear me. And maybe he'd slept crooked and had a crick in his neck, like a fellow will do sometimes. And if you happen to be all neck like Grandpa Porterfield, I expect there are days when you plain don't feel like jumping through a stupid hoop.

But Pauline had out-foxed Grandpa Porterfield. She hadn't fed him all day, and I just guess if he'd have had a stomach instead of so much neck it would have been growling something fierce. Pauline held an egg on her side of the hoop, and you could see hunger fighting disgust on Grandpa Porterfield's face.

The whole scene took my mind back to the book of Genesis, where that old serpent tempted old Eve with an apple. But in *this* case, it was Eve tempting the serpent with an egg because a snake wouldn't walk across the street for a stupid apple.

Anyway, Grandpa Porterfield finally swallowed his indignity and snaked his way across the floor to the hoop. You could see him shaking his head like he couldn't believe he was really going to do this... and then he belched. It was what you would call an inadvertent belch, but that didn't make it any less of a belch.

An "inadvertent" is when you do something you hadn't planned to and should probably apologize for, even if you're not really sorry you inadvertented.

I did not receive three perfect attendance Presbyterian Sunday School pins for nothing. That inadvertent belch was a plain act of God. If God can create the earth and the sun and the Union Pacific Railroad, He can sure as heck create a belch. Likely He even did it on a Sunday while trying not to go to sleep in church.

The point is, that belch launched Grandpa Porterfield right through Pauline's hoop and changed the world.

I couldn't stop myself from whistling and clapping; Pauline threw her arms around Grandpa Porterfield's neck, which was most of him, and kissed him on the head.

Now, if you or I had done what old Grandpa Porterfield did and got clapped at and around-the-neck hugged, I guess we would have just blushed something fierce. Well, you will never see a snake blush. Snakes are as prideful and nose-stuck-up as old lady Carmichael, goiter and all. Ask the first ten people you meet if they believe snakes are modest and they'll look at you like you're crazy.

Grandpa Porterfield caught on pretty fast. He swallowed the egg, went back around, coiled himself in front of Pauline's hoop and was ready to go again. Right through the hoop like a deadly Blue Racer striking at a Ubangi innocently tromping through the African svelte—as he went after those eggs!

Maybe Pauline was right about being able to train a snake.

Four eggs and four jumps later, Grandpa Porterfield crawled off for a nap. Pauline lit a ciggie and squinted up her eyes. I know she was seeing her name up in lights over the Big Top and the dollar bills stacking themselves in neat little piles.

16

Aunt Izzy saved me from explaining to my dad that my glasses had been broken during an Indian uprising and down-stomping. She rummaged around in her desk and found an old pair of her own glasses. They were big, round, tortoise shell things, but they worked fine for me. When I looked in the mirror, it was just like looking at Little Orphan Annie, just two big holes for eyes.

I wondered if Annie's stupid, arfing dog, Sandy, ever peed on her dictionary.

My time with Aunt Izzy was flying past. Neither of us wanted it to end. We sat at the kitchen table while Aunt Izzy prepared herself to write to my parents. She told me that old Shakespeare himself needed to be about half-snockered before he could write good, and *he* didn't even have to write to my dad. I'll say this for Aunt Izzy, there was no doubt that she was preparing to give it her best shot.

When she finally laid her pen down, she gave me a wicked grin and said, "When it comes to being a writer, old Shakespeare wouldn't amount to a pimple on my butt!" She passed the letter to me.

I skipped over the stuff about "I am fine, hope you are the same" and went right to what mattered:

> *"Young Jefferson Davis is progressing nicely for the most part. I only wish I could tell you he is completely cured of his problem. Each day I set him beside the privy with a box of matches and watch him closely. I carefully limit this time to one hour. I find if I use a longer period it is too much for him to bear. He develops the hives and the shakes and bites his fingernails to the quick. It is a terrible thing to see. Twice he opened the matchbox and removed matches, but I was right there and threw a bucket of water on him. That seems to be the best thing to do. Poor boy!*
>
> *"While I realize you must miss him terribly, in all honesty I believe you should consider leaving him under my guidance for at least two more weeks.*
>
> *"I'll admit it is not easy for a woman of my age to deal with him, but I do feel I am doing the Lord's work and pray for the strength to see him through his unhappy dysfunction."*

Aunt Izzy said it was only right and proper that I write a few words, also, then she topped off my Kool-Aid with "what makes me and Shakespeare famous."

I wrote:

> *"Dear Mother and Father, I am fine except sometimes I'd really like to burn down a privy. Hope you are the same.*
>
> *"Yr. loving son, Jefferson Davis."*

I licked the envelope. Aunt Izzy added the stamp. Then I took the letter to the mailbox and put up the little flag.

I didn't see Pauline the rest of the day or the next day either. That was all right though; Aunt Izzy kept me busy.

Her old model A Ford had got a bad shimmy in the front wheels. I joked her that she should name the car "Kate," like in the song, "I Wish I Could Shimmy Like My Sister Kate." She made an effort to laugh.

"The situation is getting a little dangerous," she told me. "I've been thinking about getting someone to come out and get the old '23 Pierce Arrow fired up again. It was running fine when your Uncle Willard died."

That was the best news ever!

I could see myself pulling that beautiful car into Pauline's driveway and saying "Pauline, get Grandpa Porterfield and we'll go for a quick spin and observe the verdant countryside."

See, "verdant" just means green, but a fellow wouldn't dare say it unless he was driving a Pierce Arrow.

And Pauline would get old Grandpa Porterfield coiled up and comfortable and then close the door with that quiet, Pierce Arrow "snick."

"Gotta ciggie?" I'd ask.

"'Course I do, dummy," she'd say. "And I've got my dad's silver Ronson lighter too."

And we'd light up and Pauline would blow the smoke out her nose, and I'd act like there wasn't anything special about that. But there was, because when I tried it always made me sneeze. And you'll never in the world catch a fellow who drives a Price Arrow sneezing.

Anyway, Aunt Izzy and I started cleaning the dirt

and the bird poop off the car. It took most of the day. I kept a close watch on Aunt Izzy from the corner of my eye to see if she noticed my disturbance of the old treasure trunk with the French ladies in it. She didn't give it a glance. I wasn't near finished with those French ladies. They were my best education potential, and potentials often stop working when adults find out about them.

Until it was cleaned up, I hadn't realized how beautiful that car really was. Aunt Izzy called Sam's Garage, and Sam promised he'd come out first thing in the morning with some gasoline and a new battery.

Aunt Izzy fixed bacon and tomato sandwiches for supper. She was a great one for explaining what the proper wine was to use with each food. She said the Count of Monte Cristo always drank dandelion wine with his bacon and tomato sandwiches, and I figured he ought to know.

It's pretty hard to get to sleep when you know that tomorrow you may be amazing the world by speeding down the road in a Pierce Arrow. I wished to gosh old Purdy Grundy and Pinky Smail could be there to see me. Their old livers would be turning green just wishing they were me and had an aunt who owned a Pierce Arrow.

I guess now they'll stop razzing me about having three Presbyterian Sunday School perfect attendance buttons!

I'll say, "Boys, if you knew your Bible you'd know it says, 'Suffer the little children to come unto me.' Maybe if you'd sat through three years of Presbyterian Sunday School, you'd have suffered enough to have an aunt with a Pierce Arrow!"

I went to sleep knowing if I ever got a dollar bill, I'd put it in the good old collection plate.

Next morning Aunt Izzy fixed fried okra for breakfast and I asked her what kind of wine we should
be drinking with it. She told me most people who
eat fried okra for breakfast just slug it down with
straight whiskey, but we had a big day ahead of us
so we'd stick to coffee.

Aunt Izzy still had her hands up to her elbows in
the breakfast dishwater when we heard the Sam's
Garage truck scrunching up the driveway.

"Would you go show him where the car is, Jeffie?
And be polite."

I strolled out the front door, trying for all the
world to look like a fellow would stroll whose great
aunt owned a Pierce Arrow.

"Good morning," I told him. I offered him my
hand and said, "I'm Jefferson Davis Johnson, the
boy whose own aunt owns the Pierce Arrow, which
is in need of repair."

He took my hand solemnly, and said, "I'm Sam."

"And what might your last name be, Sam?" I
sounded for all the world like my dad.

"Why, it's 'Garage.' See, just like it says on my
truck." He gestured toward the side panel and gave
me a look, then added, "It's a French name."

Holy cow! I should have known.

I showed him where to drive his truck up close to
the barn and led him inside.

"Well hell yes," he said, "I remember this car. Old
Willard bought it new about a year before he died."
He walked all around it and said "Still looks just like
new!"

"Yes, sir," I told him, "It's a Pierce Arrow. It belongs to my own great aunt now. I'll be glad to help
you work on it."

He thought that over for a couple of seconds, and
I could tell he appreciated my thoughtfulness.

"I can tell right now I'm going to need a left-handed, double-ventilated whatsomedooger. I know your great aunt doesn't have one. I'd just take it mighty kindly if you'd ask around at your neighbors' and see if you can borrow one. Won't need it but just for a few minutes." I was off like a shot.

I ran all the way up to Pauline's to see if she had inherited her dead father's left-handed, double-ventilated whatsomedooger but she stopped me at the front fence. She told me she was teaching Grandpa Porterfield a super new trick, and I couldn't see it yet. I told her this was a dang emergency and she told me to go stick beans up my nose, so I told her to stick beans up her own stupid nose and took off running down toward Indigenous Dennis's place.

I found Mr. Aborigine Eugene scratching through the tall grass in his backyard. He didn't look happy; and when I explained that I needed a left-handed double-ventilated whatsomedooger right away and that Pauline had told me to go stick beans up my nose he didn't look as happy as before I told him.

"I've looked all over the goddamned state of Kansas without finding my goddamned hatchet!" he shouted. "How do you expect me to find a goddamned ventiflooger?"

I could have told him his hatchet was buried with the cucumbers, and I could have told him to stick a goddamned bean up his nose but, once again, my good Presbyterian instincts won out. I just thanked him and ran back home.

I just guess Mr. Sam's Garage was about as fine a mechanic as ever came down the pike! There, backed out of the barn and purring like a kitten, was the grandest sight I'd ever seen.

The sunlight glittered off those long, funnel-shaped headlights that tapered into the fenders, and

Henry Ford and Mr. Chevrolet would have cut their grandma's throats to be able make a car like that.

Aunt Izzy stood with Mr. Sam's Garage, happy tears running down her cheeks. "Lord, I just wish my brother, Willard, could be here to see this day!" she kept saying.

"Bring it in tomorrow and we'll put new tires and a new fan-belt on," Sam's told her.

I grabbed hold of a small sapling to keep from floating plumb off the Earth.

17

First thing after breakfast, we drove to Sam's Garage in Armageddon. I'd just as well not bothered to brush my hair because the Pierce Arrow was what Aunt Izzy called a "breezer." That meant it had no top except for a canvas one which you could pull up if it rained. Aunt Izzy sang all the way and said she only wished she'd got this old car out sooner.

I wanted to ask Aunt Izzy to blow the horn as we went past Pauline's house but, fortunately, I remembered her cruel and wicked treatment of me when all I wanted was to borrow a left-handed, double-ventilated whatsomedooger. See, that's why it's so easy to hate girls. But I knew that some sweet day she would come begging for a ride in the Pierce Arrow and I would tell her, "Pauline, just go stick beans up your nose!"

While Sam's put on the new tires and the new fan belt, Aunt Izzy and I walked a couple blocks to a hardware store and bought a can of Neatsfoot Oil. She said those black leather seats were so dry they might crack and, "One must not have *cracked* seats in one's Pierce Arrow."

On our trip home, what with new tires and a new fan-belt, Aunt Izzy showed me "What this baby can do." The wind whooshed by and it was almost too noisy to talk, but I made Aunt Izzy understand it was like riding a cloud through heaven. She hollered back that if there were any angels around, they had better grab their harps and get the hell out of the way! Aunt Izzy couldn't be a Presbyterian in a million years.

Back home we were greeted by every single one of Aunt Izzy's Rudolph cats. Aunt Izzy blowed and blowed the horn, but I guess if you have nine lives you don't mind losing a few for the honor of being squashed by a Pierce Arrow.

We worked on the car the whole afternoon, Aunt Izzy washing and waxing it, and me rubbing Neatsfoot oil into the leather seats. Even old George Washington would have been proud to ride in that beauty.

Next morning, early, we climbed into the Pierce Arrow again. Aunt Izzy turned the key, toed the starter, and a tiger started purring under the hood. Aunt Izzy was wearing a beaded dress and a cloche hat which looked like a thimble turned upside down on her head. Around her neck she wore "my Isadora Duncan suicide scarf." My own head, she'd slicked down with Vaseline so's I'd look like "The Sheik of Arab E."

Aunt Izzy had taken the time to open the rumble seat, though it beat me why she would—since there was just the two of us.

"Gets mighty tiresome being all alone in that old hideout," she explained. I didn't ask any more questions and I didn't look. I knew there would be a train-robber-killer-cookie-baker riding right behind me.

Aunt Izzy was all giggly, and promised we'd speed around Armageddon and show those rubes how the *good* life used to be.

Well, we'd barely started down the driveway when Aunt Izzy jammed on the breaks and said, "Damn! It's another covey of those crazy WCTUers."

All I saw was five or six ladies dressed up in hats and good clothes, carrying Bibles. I must have looked confused. "Women's Christen Temperance Union," she expounded. Then I understood.

They were being led by a couple of Carry A. Nationites carrying hatchets, coming right at us, looking serious as a prairie fire.

"Somehow they've got the idea that I take an occasional little drink, and about once a month they come and flop down on their knees and try to pray me onto the wagon," Aunt Izzy whispered.

"Well," I told her, "I just guess when they see you in this good old Pierce Arrow, they'll forget all about putting you on a stupid wagon."

But Aunt Izzy wasn't listening. She was planning her next move.

All of the sudden an adenoid-blistering, bellowing, screaming "rebel yell" rose up from the rumble seat.

Aunt Izzy jammed down on the gas pedal. We shot forward, and I saw why the car was called an "arrow." She aimed the radiator cap right at the belly buttons of the Nationites, and the whole flock screamed, waved their Bibles and their hatchets, and scattered like the sands of time.

It was an adroit move, and it out-adroited those ladies slicker than snot. An "adroit" is when you make your Pierce Arrow go faster than a Nationite's hatchet.

Now you understand, at first I had no idea what

that terrible sound was. Later, "in her cups," as the fellow says, Aunt Izzy explained it to me.

"Just feel lucky old Jesse softened that yell down for the benefit of those WCTUers and Carry A. Nationites," she told me. "Coming from right behind you like that, a real Rebel Yell would have melted your ear wax. The Free Staters and the abolitionists never got off that easy. They flat out got their old blood curdled!

"After he got killed and took early retirement, Jesse honed that Rebel Yell to where it was just like a fiery comet with barbs and all manner of sticky-thingies along the edges. Sometimes at night you can hear him practicing up there in that old coal mine hideout. That's when the lions and the lambs and the porcupines and the dove cotes all crawl into their little tunnels and lie down together."

It all sounded so Bibleistic. There couldn't be a doubt about it. Heck fire, it got me thinking.

If I can listen to old Jesse James a few times and practice enough myself, I can teach that yell to my dad. Then, when the Day of Rapture comes and all the Presbyterians are going through the Pearly Gates, my dad can whirl around and thumb his nose at the poor old Methodists and Baptists and Congregationalites and give them the Rebel Yell. That'll make my dad feel like a million dollars, and give all those losers a scenic view of their world to come. If there's one thing I know for sure, it's that a fellow ought to honor his father—and his mother, if he's got one who is a nose thumber.

But I have got off the track. I started to tell you about me and Aunt Izzy going Pierce Arrowing into Armageddon.

I cannot sincerely say if the immortal spirit of Jesse James had stayed in the rumble seat or if he got out to spook the WCTUers. At any rate, if he stayed he had enough sense to not do the rebel yell when the officer stopped us at the corner of 6th and Perdition, in the old part of town.

I'm still not sure just why he stopped us, but he looked the Pierce Arrow over pretty good and he looked Aunt Izzy over and he looked me, with my supremely Vaselined hair, over. Then he asked, "Ma'am, I wonder if you would be so good as to tell me what year this is?"

Aunt Izzy blinked her eyelashes a couple times, and said, "Why, certainly, suh. It's 1923. Now, y'all knew that, didn't you? You silly boy. And this is my brand new Pierce Arrow, and this is my little brother, Jefferson Davis."

Well, that policeman knew his manners because he blinked his eyelashes a couple of times, too, and said, "Ma'am, I wonder if you would be so good as to tell me who is the president of the United States?"

Aunt Izzy waved her hand in front of her face like she was brushing away a fly, and said, "Now you're joshing me, aren't you, you silly thing. As you well know our new president is Mr. Calvin Coolidge. Mind you, I don't much hold with Republicans after what they did to us in the South."

"Ma'am, does the name Franklin D. Roosevelt ring any bells with you?"

"Well, now, ah cain't say as it does. Live around here, does he?"

Then that policeman looked right at me and said, "Young man, do you know what year this is?" I looked him right back straight in the eye, and said, "Yes suh, ah reckons it's just like my sister, Miss Great Aunt Queen Isabella of Spain says. It's 1923. You seen any ostriches lately?"

Right then Aunt Izzy broke in and said, "Now,

Officer, I expect you just stopped us so's to sell us tickets to the Policeman's Ball, so I'll buy two."

"Lady, Lady..." he said, pushing his policeman's hat back on his head, "Policemen in Armageddon don't have balls, we have an annual raffle." Aunt Izzy gave him a sympathetic look but kept her mouth shut.

"Now look, Lady, this time I'm just going to give you a warning."

Aunt Izzy interrupted again and said, "Oh, you old joker, you! Ah reckon ah know what your li'l ol' joke 'guine be. Y'all's gone say, 'Don't take any wooden nickels, y'hear.' I heard that un a million times! Anyway, I gotta go now, mighty nice a talk'n with y'all..."

Well, Aunt Izzy took off like a turpentined cat, and when I looked back that policeman was sitting on the curb holding his head in his hands. When you stop to think about it, I just expect city policemen do get awful tired, standing on those hard old streets all day.

Aunt Izzy was grinning like a Chessie Cat. "I say it as one who shouldn't, Jeffie, but there's not a man in the world who can resist my 'Po li'l South'n Girl' routine. We flat bamfloozled that copper! We hoodwinked him and pulled the wool over his eyes. You did a good job, too, Jeffie. I expect he's still sitting there wondering why he never sees any ostriches!"

We made a grand tour of good old Armageddon, likely going faster than Christians should. But I'll tell you, we were having a *time*. After a while, Aunt Izzy suggested we go over to F.W.Woolworth's and splurge on a bowl of chop suey.

"Maybe it's a little early?" she wondered.

"No, ma'am," I told her. "Anybody ever asks, I tell 'em, 'Never too early for some F.W.Woolworth chop suey!'"

If she regretted ruffling my supremely Vaselined hair with her fingers, she didn't say. What she said was, "You're just the cat's pajamas, Jeffie. *The* cat's pajamas!

Back home we wiped the dust and smashed bugs off the car until it sparkled like new again. By the time we had everything just perfect, Aunt Izzy declared herself too tired to think straight; I admitted I was too. We suppered on leftovers, piled the dishes in the sink, and flopped down by the radio to relax. But, before the tubes had warmed up enough for the whistling and greezling and popping to stop, the phone rang—one short, two longs, and one short.

Aunt Izzy put the receiver to her ear and gave out a cheery "Hello," which quickly turned into a sour, "Oh, hello, Little Willard."

I think I told you, "Little Willard" is what Aunt Izzy always called my father so she could tell him from her brother who was also a Willard, but a bigger one, but then Little Willard grew big, and regular Willard became dead Willard, even though nobody called him that but she still calls my father Little Willard because it's hard to break the habit.

When she finally said, "Alright, Little Willard, we'll look for you Saturday morning," and hung up, her face looked older and sadder.

"Your father says they now have all the indoor plumbing installed and it's safe for you to come home whether you are cured or not. I guess our fun is about over, Jeffie. I'm sorry."

She turned the radio back on, but "The Great Gildersleeve" didn't seem very funny, and "Red Skelton" didn't seem very funny. Even "Amos and Andy" wasn't funny.

Aunt Izzy said a bad word and suggested we just

turn in for the night. I felt so downhearted I didn't even say, "I wouldn't have in my hand what you had in your mouth."

Then she said it again.

In the morning I woke remembering this would be close to the last time I would sleep in this bed—in this house. So I knew I would never sleep again. Not in my own bed, not in any bed. There just wasn't another bed in the world as comfortable as this one. I tried one of Aunt Izzy's bad words, but it didn't help.

When I glumphed my way downstairs to breakfast, there was Aunt Izzy, cheerful as could be, singing "Happy Days Are Here Again."

I couldn't help it, the tears rolled down my cheeks. She was glad I was going—glad to be rid of me.

But then, she put her arms around me and said, "Don't cry, Jeffie. It's going to be alright. We still have almost a week, and I've got a plan."

And what a plan she had!

"But, first of all, I figure we should have all the fun we can for the rest of the time you're here. What would you really, really, really like to do?"

I took the last spoonful of my boiled Grape Nuts and drank the last of the sugar milk from the bowl. I knew I was taking a big chance, but I swallowed a couple times, then started, "You promise you won't get mad?" I asked.

"I promise," she said.

I blurted it out. "Well, I guess what I'd really like to do is see the old Jesse James Coal Mine."

She puckered her mouth up, just ever so slightly, and thought a few seconds.

"All right," she said. "I'll go up right now and make sure it's all right."

Just how she planned to "make sure," I daren't ask.

She was gone a while, for sure, and I was beginning to wonder if something bad had happened. By the time she got back I had the dishes done and the table scrubbed 'til it sparkled.

"He said he'd be glad to see you. Said he figured you'd sneak up on your own, but I told him you'd promised not to, and you were too good a boy to go back on your word."

Well, I was glad she thought well of me, but I wasn't too sure I was glad a train-robber-killer-outlaw ghost wanted me to come to his hideout. It's a whale of a lot easier to be brave when you know you aren't allowed to do a thing than it is when nobody cares a snap if you do.

Aunt Izzy filled the lantern with coal oil and we started off, moving uphill through the stick-tights and the devil claws, with a whole-State-of-Kansas-worth of Rudolph cats flittering around our feet.

Wasn't much to look at from the outside. Weeds grown up all around. Just a dark old hole in the side of a little hill. Aunt Izzy called it an "adit." Looked like it didn't want to be there, and wouldn't, except for the heavy timbers holding it—against its will.

If I'd been the sheriff, with my posse riding behind me, and knew that old Jesse James was right behind that black hole waiting for me, I'd of likely pointed off the other way and said, "Well, looky there, boys, ain't that a double-breasted, red-headed female whiffletree flying there?"

Aunt Izzy looked to be right at home. She lit the lantern, looked at me, and said, "You sure you want to do this, Jeffie?"

Hot damn, I wish she hadn't said that.

We stepped inside.

I'll tell you this, I'm not sure that old lantern liked

being there either. The dark was pushy. Seemed like the lantern didn't want the light wandering off and leaving it alone. Finally, after a forever, Aunt Izzy turned the wick up and the dark backed away a little.

It wasn't at all like I thought a coal mine would be; it just seemed like a big room. Aunt Izzy explained it had been one huge thick vein of coal, and when the miners reached the other side, it had petered out into dirt again.

When my eyes got used to the dark I could see a couple of little crawly-hole tunnels leading off from the opposite sides of the room, maybe to nowhere... but maybe to somewhere.

And there, sure enough, just like Aunt Izzy had told me days ago, was Jesse James's kitchen: an old Hoosier kitchen cabinet and a cast iron cooking stove, looking sad and dusty and cold.

At the other end, the far end, of the coal-room there was a sort of shelf, like a stage, about a foot off the floor. Aunt Izzy said that was where Great Uncle Willard had stopped digging. On that little stage sat a plate of warm "Train Robber cookies."

"Jesse's glad you came," Aunt Izzy said quietly.

18

Fortunately, Aunt Izzy hadn't sworn me to secrecy about our visit to the Jesse James Hideout and Coal Mine. Despite the fact that I still hated Pauline... some...for her rude treatment of me when I asked for the simple loan of a left-handed, double-ventilated whatsomedooger, I was about to bust, wanting to tell her about my adventure. Out of Christian charity I decided to give her one more chance, because she probably couldn't help acting like a girl.

As it turned out, she seemed glad to see me and never even mentioned beans or noses. With girls you just never know!

Anyway, I found her in her barn with Grandpa Porterfield and a little basket of eggs. She was just finishing tying twisted hay around the edge of her nail keg hoop, and she looked considerable happier than Grandpa Porterfield did.

"We gotta go outside for this," she said.

Pauline led me and Grandpa Porterfield out to a bare spot of ground and commanded Grandpa Porterfield, "Get ready!" She held the hoop on the end of a stick, lit the hay 'til it burned all around, and said, "Jump, Grandpa Porterfield. Jump. Show us what you can do!"

It was plain to me that this was not the first time Grandpa Porterfield had jumped through a flaming hoop. I would go so far as to say that Grandpa Porterfield had become a "ham." He didn't swallow hard, he didn't blink his eyes; he just flew through that old flaming hoop like it was redemption day at the Pearly Gates.

Old Pauline's eyes shined. She patted Grandpa Porterfield on the head and said, "Take a bow, Grandpa Porterfield." At the same time, she gave me a motion to clap, and I just guess I did!

I expect if I live to be thirty-five, I'll never see a grander sight than that snake's bow. Grandpa Porterfield coiled himself into a neat little spring-shape, raised his head, and belched. He looked proud as Jenny Lind, the Swedish Nightingale, and I'll bet anything I've got she couldn't have belched any louder.

Pauline plopped down on the ground beside me and pulled out two ciggies and her Ronson lighter. Blowing smoke out her nose like a happy dragon, she leaned close to me and said, "I'm as good as rich, and you may kiss me."

Well now, see, I wasn't exactly clear on how to go about kissing a *poor* girl; I wasn't about to trust to beginner's luck with an almost rich one. To be perfectly honest, I also didn't feel it necessary to mention that I'd rather kiss the dang snake.

Be that as it may, Pauline forgot all about kissing when I let go with a loud, fake cough. She backed right off and told me I was the most unefficient smoker she'd ever seen. She said I should either learn to smoke right or see if I could learn to chew gum without choking on it.

Anyway, she was too full of her new glory to waste much time on me. She had her future all mapped out and seemed about ready to buy herself a wheelbarrow to carry all her money to the bank.

"You wait," she told me. "First circus comes through here, I'll show them my trained snake act, and I'll be gone, gone, gone! I'll go all over the world wearing a spangly dress, and Grandpa Porterfield will belch and jump through the fiery hoop and pluck eggs out of my hand, and the old Queen of England will say, 'Sumbich, Miss The Amazing Pauline, I'd sure like to see that again!'

"Then I'll curtsy like old Shirley Temple, and I'll say, "Well, why the hell not? But it'll cost you another golden tiara and four more diadems.

"And the old Queen of England will say, 'You reckon I could feed that Grandpa Porterfield snake one of them eggs?' And I'll say, 'Be all right, but careful he don't bite you.' And old Queen will say, 'Shit, girl, I been bit by Prime Ministers with bigger teeth than that.'"

Well see, a little of that Queen of England talk, and a little of that "Gay Paree" talk of getting old Too Loose LaTrek to paint her picture with her spangly skirt pulled up above her knees—but without the scabs—well, a little goes a long ways.

Shoot, my own adventure was about to pop its buttons! So I told her about going to the Jesse James Hideout and Coal Mine, and the tunnels that went off into black and no living person knew what was at the end of them.

"Most likely," I said, "it's old dead bones guarding a untold treasure."

I told her about the warm Train Robber cookies,

fresh out of an ice cold oven. Then I remembered the little stage-like place, and the idea hit me. That little stage would be the perfect place!

I laid it all out for Pauline. The sign would say, *"The Miss Amazing Pauline,"* and in smaller letters under that, *"and her deadly and dangerous belching, egg-sucking snake, Grandpa Porterfield."*

I told her how we'd put about seventeen lanterns around the stage, all shining on her and her spangly dress, and how that fiery hoop would just scare people to death there in the dark! Then, when Grandpa Porterfield jumped through the flame, she could hold him up and show that his eyebrows weren't even singed, and...I'd just as well saved my breath.

She was a girl. She was going to run off with the circus, whether or no.

I guess we must have argued for an hour, back and forth and back and forth. I don't know why I even bothered because I knew she was a girl. But, finally, I wore her down.

What I did was "prevail." A prevail is when you get someone so sick of you that they say "Aw, to hell with it," and let you have your way.

The next thing to do was a prevail on Aunt Izzy and Jesse James to let us use the hideout-coal mine for a Beejew theater.

As it turned out, Aunt Izzy didn't take any prevailing at all. She said the snake show would fit right in with her plan, and that Jesse would probably be glad for a little excitement, too.

I sat down at the kitchen table and composed what they call a "press release" for *The Buffalo County Trans-Weekly Disciplinarian* and planned a big poster for the front yard:

→ **Big Show** ←
Coming Sataurday to a coal mine near you!

Featuring
→ **Miss Amazing Pauline** ←

with the
Dangerous and Deadly
→ **Grandpa Porterfield*** ←

He jumps through fiery hoops!
He sucks eggs! He belches!

Location: The Jesse James Hideout and Coal Mine Co.
Formerly owned by the posthumous **Mr. Great Uncle Willard Johnson**. Now owned by his sister, **Miss Queen Isabella of Spain Johnson**, who also got his Pierce Arrow and looks like Louise Brooks because she got her hair cut.

Time: Right after the privy burns down

Come one—Come all!
Admission: 10 cents
(free Train Robber Cookie for each paid admitant)

***a snake**

Aunt Izzy said I'd done good, and admitted I would likely be Robert Louis Stevenson when I grew up.

19

When Friday morning arrived most of the work for Aunt Izzy's plan was done. I'd taken Pauline up to the mine and she was near overcome by bliss. She wanted to crawl into the little tunnels, but I told her we weren't allowed, and she told me, "If you're afraid, then I'll go first."

Then she decided she couldn't go first because I would see her underpants and I told her I wouldn't look at her stupid underpants because I was Presbyterian and she said "Sumbich! Just forget it." So we did.

Now, I'll tell you this about cleaning a coal mine: you can't! Pauline and I did the best we could, but we raised such a dust we had to get out until it settled. We set lanterns around the "stage," and Pauline practiced standing up there saying "Jump, Grandpa Porterfield. Jump."

Aborigine Eugene and Indigenous Dennis had cleared a path through the stick-tights and devil claws so, except for an occasional, inadvertent just-passing-through rattlesnake, our customers could get to the mine easy—except for the Rudolph cats.

Aunt Izzy had bought a bunch of lemons and made enough lemonade to feed the multitude, if one showed up.

She also brought out a sign she had made:

Wet Paint
Please use back door

She hung that on the front screen door, and the two of us carried some old boards and laid them across the front steps. Next we gathered all the old newspapers we could find and filled the privy with them.

We were both up at the crack of dawn on Saturday. Breakfast over, dishes done. Indigenous Dennis showed up and had a cup of coffee with us. Aunt Izzy added a little something special to both of theirs.

Aunt Izzy stationed me at the end of the driveway, far enough down so I could see the highway about half a mile away. I would be able to spot my dad long before he made the turn toward Aunt Izzy's. Indigenous Dennis had soaked the privy down with coal oil and stood ready with a box of matches.

I'll tell you, it seemed to take forever, and I'll probably go to hell for even thinking it, but I don't guess I was ever so glad to see my dad as when he finally made the turn off the highway about 11:00 a.m.

I shouted to Aunt Izzy and she shouted to Indigenous Dennis. Then we hid.

My dad pulled his Hudson Terraplane up close to the house. It was new, it was shiny, some of it sparkled...but compared to the Pierce Arrow it looked like an ugly, old, worn-out shoe.

Aunt Izzy had warned me there was a chance her

plan might not work. My dad might stay longer than she hoped. Just in case, she had rummaged around and found the forty-year-old lemon she'd used making lemonade for "Little Willard" since he was a kid.

My dad was half way to the front door when he noticed the boards blocking the steps and then the Wet Paint sign. He had just started to go around the house when it happened.

Well, look at me! I've spent half my life learning a new word everyday and the best I can say is "it happened!" Still and all, I'm not really sure of everything that did happen.

There's a goofy old man in Epic who, when the Armistice Day parade goes by, holds up his fist and hollers "REMEMBER THE MAINE!" I figured, when he got word of this, he'd be shouting "REMEMBER THE PRIVY!"

First there was a loud PLOOOF, and the air quivered, it seemed to suck itself in, then blow itself out again. My dad staggered backwards. Clouds of black smoke billowed up from the privy and bits of flaming wood shingles rained down. From the back of the house Aunt Izzy let out a scream that might curdle your adenoids, "Oh my God! He's done it again!"

Aunt Izzy raced toward my dad, still screaming... but it wasn't the Aunt Izzy he knew. It wasn't the family matriarch he'd feared and respected all his life. It was some seventy year old crazy woman with short-cut hair that looked like a football helmet. It was Louise Brooks grown as old as King Tut. He spun around and made for the Hudson Terraplane as fast as his short, fat little legs could take him.

And right behind him, fast as a tornado and just as stormy, came Aunt Izzy.

"Come back, Little Willard." she shouted, "Come back! I thought he was cured! Come back and take your wicked son home with you. He has trampled my inalienable rights into the dust and burned down my privy. You come right back and pay me every penny it will cost to rebuild!"

But the Hudson Terraplane roared. The tires spewed gravel until it pinged off the house.

I'm not saying my dad was a coward, not in any way, shape or form. I believe he just needed a little time to think things over.

My dad was gone, but what seemed to me like everybody in Buffalo County began arriving. I mean no disrespect, but I just guess if old Jesus thought He had a lot of people at the Sermon on the Mount, well, He should have tried burning down a privy!

Not only that, when the privy was mostly gone Aunt Izzy started herding everybody up to the old mine. Seemed a lot of them had always wanted to have a look at where Jesse James had hung out.

And I just don't guess my poster hurt anything either.

Indigenous Dennis stood at the adit and collected the dimes. He also got a quarter each for little chunks of coal that Pauline had put in a basket with a sign saying: "Jesse James peed on each of these."

Pauline looked better than you could ever believe. She had brushed her hair and that, on its own recognizance, was worth the price of admission. She was all decked out in a pink dress covered with Christmas tree tinsel, and if she didn't look as good as a French lady then I don't know what to tell you.

Grandpa Porterfield turned out to be the star of the show. He belched and sucked eggs and jumped through that flaming hoop like a trooper. Several people wanted to buy him, but Pauline just told them to go cook a radish.

A few times the lanterns flickered as a cool breeze seemed to move around the room, but I think I was the only one who noticed it.

We had to do three shows that day to accommodate all the people, and some asked when we would be doing it again.

With the last of our attendees headed for home, we all trudged down the hill as tired as we'd ever been.

Except for Aunt Izzy. She said she reckoned she'd stay and visit awhile.

When Aunt Izzy and I faced each other at breakfast next day, we couldn't get over yesterday's success, and we also couldn't help remembering the way my dad had made the dash for his car. We both started laughing all over again.

Then she pulled a sober face and said, "You know we should not be laughing, young man. That was a mean trick we pulled on your poor father, and we should be ashamed."

"Ok, I'm ashamed," I said, bowing my head and looking contrite.

A "contrite" is how you better look if you've done something that will take more than just a "sorry" to get you out of trouble. See, a sorry will get you by if you've dribbled the gravy on the tablecloth, or pooped in church. But if you've done a mean thing to your mom or dad you dang well be ready to do a contrite. Still and all, if you happen to have a mouthful of milk and, at the same time you have an Aunt Izzy glowering a fake glower at you...it plain won't work.

And I did, and it didn't.

And we started out laughing all over again.

"Well, Jeffie, the way I see it is this, we most likely won't see Little Willard again until school starts. Of

course, there's always the chance he'll call the sheriff and have him put you in the Orphan's Home. On
the other hand, he may be so embarrassed he'll just
go hide in the Orphan's Home himself."

A few days later we got a letter from my father,
in it was a check for $15 and a note apologizing for
leaving so quickly. He said he'd remembered he had
not locked the safe at the bank. He asked Aunt Izzy
if she could keep me till the end of summer, and
then added a P.S. that they might want me back
then.

Aunt Izzy seems to be spending a lot of time up
at the old mine, but first chance she gets she's going
to teach me how to drive that good old Pierce Arrow.

I just guess that'll about be the cat's pajamas.
The cat's pajamas!

About the Author

Max Yoho has established himself as a witty writer from the nation's Heartland. He has published award winning novels, poetry, short stories and essays. A growing list of fans enjoy his offbeat sense of humor and mind boggling leaps of logic which leave readers laughing out loud.

Max is a lifelong Kansan. Born in 1934, he lived in Colony until he was ten. His next home was Atchison, then Topeka, where he graduated from Topeka High School and attended Washburn University.

He worked 38 years as a machinist. After retiring in 1992, Max developed what had started as a short story into his first novel, *The Revival*. Published in 2001, the novel won the 2002 J. Donald Coffin Memorial Book Award of Kansas Authors Club. A second novel, *Tales from Comanche County*, grew from Max's memories of his great aunt and great uncle. Max's poems, essays and short stories are collected in *Felicia, These Fish Are Delicious*. *The Moon Butter Route*, a novel about bootlegging in Southeastern Kansas, was among the first books listed as Kansas Notable Books by the Kansas Center for the Book. This book also won the 2007 J. Donald Coffin Memorial Book Award of Kansas Authors Club. *With the Wisdom of Owls* was published in 2010.

In *Me and Aunt Izzy* Max pays another visit to the world of challenges in growing up, seasoned with a twist of nostalgia.

www.ingramcontent.com/pod-product-compliance
Lightning Source LLC
Chambersburg PA
CBHW051840170626
46807CB00003B/1272